RED PEPPER RETURNS

RED PEPPER RETURNS

Grace S. Richmond

Author of THE LISTENING POST
RED PEPPER BURNS, *etc.*

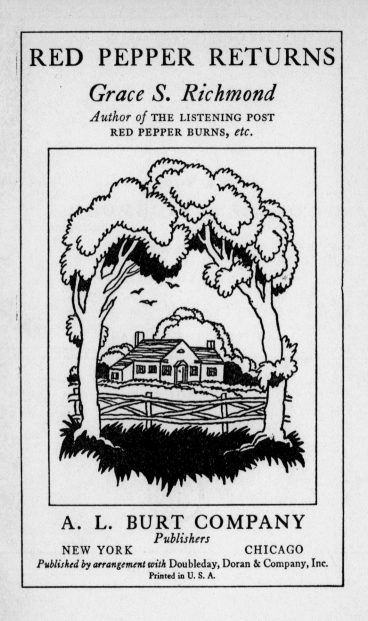

A. L. BURT COMPANY

Publishers

NEW YORK   CHICAGO

Published by arrangement with Doubleday, Doran & Company, Inc.

Printed in U. S. A.

PRINTED AT THE *Country Life Press*, GARDEN CITY, N. Y., U. S. A.

RED PEPPER RETURNS

TO
WILLIAM SEAMAN BAINBRIDGE, M. D.

LETTER from Dr. Redfield Pepper Burns to his sister Anne, Mrs. Richard Sutherland, in reply to a cable and a following letter telling him what has happened.

DEAR ANNE:

Well, of course, it's tough luck, spoiling a swell motor trip through France and Italy with a spill like that. Sorry you're not over here, where I could look after you. Meanwhile, you're in the best of hands, in that sanitarium, and you'll come along all right, if not as fast as your own idea of these matters would suggest. The incident certainly does interrupt your and Dick's here-to-day-and-to-morrow-a-thousand-miles-away schedule of travel. Too bad he can't stay with you—and yet, just as well, maybe. Husbands get impatient and expect—as you do

—such a job of convalescence to be done up in a week or two. Whereas, if you take my advice, you'll settle in and give yourself a chance to catch up with yourself in other ways than getting a few bones knit. You've been playing hard and fast with that excellent constitution of yours this good while, Anne. Expecting because you weighed a nice one hundred and forty and looked like a thirty-year-old instead of —what is it now, Anne?—you could keep going like a whirling dervish indefinitely. Yes, I know, my child! But if I've kept up the pace it's because I'd probably die—or somebody would—if I didn't. Let's not go into that.

Yes, of course I'll write to you often. So will Ellen. I'm not much on letters, but if my hasty scrawls will be any consolation to you for not being able to get on to Paris and plunge into an orgy of buying and beautifying, I'll consider it a duty to send 'em. Cheer up, Anne. You might have had a broken nose—or a broken back—out of that smash. As it is, with your pretty features intact, you can afford to lie by and watch the doctors and nurses keep up a routine that would floor you in a week. You live on a round of so-called pleasure, doing what you want to. They live on exercise, duty, *tragedy, with an occasional touch of comedy to make it all bearable, yet mostly doing what they don't want to. Just the same, you're a good sport, Anne, if marrying a rich man did keep you eating cream when you ought to have been drinking butter-milk. You'll come through this and be none the worse.*

I'm just off for Baltimore. Ellen's gone down to South Carolina for one of her visits to her few relatives—and to get away from me. You know her little game. It works, I have to admit it. She's been gone only twenty-four hours, but with the young-sters away at school, and a lucky lull in operative cases, I can't stand it around here—must get to one of Jack Leaver's clinics and see his latest modern miracle working on that ever fascinating, baffling, unpredictable, four-dimensional challenge, the human body. When I get through with mine I hope its Maker will give me a chance to dissect it—in the floodlights of the Hereafter.

Gloomy-sounding note to stop on? Not at all. But here's a livelier: a message from Bob, to whom I telephoned the news about you. "Tell Aunt Anne to find herself a handsome Italian doctor to make eyes at—she knows how, and it will help pass the time."

Superfluous advice, I call that, Anne. You've un-
doubtedly got one with his hand on his heart right
now.

*   That's where mine is, too, in spite of my insults.*

RED.

I

R<small>ED</small>, there's just one thing that's puzzled me about you, all these years."

"Only one?"

"Well, this seems the most pressing, at the moment: . . . *When do you sleep?*"

Dr. Burns, sitting on the edge of his office desk, glanced up from the page of a magazine devoted to the promotion of interest in aviation. "You know, Jim," he said to his next-door neighbor, James Macauley, "I'm pretty sure I've bought the right ship. But between all the different types of the smaller ships, which one is going to get me there the quickest and also be most foolproof, is still uncertain. Now, this——"

"I've been put off and put off," declared his friend, "on the answer to that question, and now I'm going to have it. When do you sleep?"

Burns replied absently, his gaze back on the picture of a famous tri-motored plane, just arrived from across the Atlantic: "I gave up night work long ago, as you know perfectly well. So why——"

"Last night," persisted the questioner, "Martha says she heard your car go out at two-thirty in the morning."

"She contradicts herself. Night and morning are not interchangeable terms."

"They are with you. And the night before—and pretty nearly every night—lights pop on in your office. You slide out—I know you do."

Burns stood up and shook his fist at Macauley. "You're the doggonedest inquisitive, interfering, impertinent neighbor I have," he asserted, "except Arthur Chester, on the other side. Both of you drive me to lying in your impudent faces. Well, now, here's the truth. Two weeks ago you got me up at 1 A. M. for a pain in your neck——"

"You hadn't gone to bed."

"And the night before that, towards three o'clock, Ches got a scare because he thought he'd given Win a dose of benzoin instead of ginger and came tearing over. As if it made a pin's difference which he gave her. *Night work!*"

"Well, you wouldn't want to let your best friends die, would you?"

"The town is filled," explained Red, "with people who also consider themselves best friends and therefore exceptions to the rule. As for your infernal question, When do I sleep? I sleep when I'm not awake, and that's what every mother's son of us does, and let's quit talking about it. When I get my pilot's license and don't have to depend on Norton, I shall probably fly all night, every night, for the fun of it, because I'm too busy in the day-time. And you and Art Chester'll be out on the landing field among the bright lights, when you ought to be in bed, begging to go along."

"You bet we will," agreed James Macauley, with a grin.

He knew well enough he would never get any nearer an answer to his question, because there wasn't any answer.

2

DR. REDFIELD PEPPER BURNS—he was accustomed to sign his orders and prescriptions simply "R. P. Burns," and his friends called him "Red Pepper," but we are giving him his full designation at the start—climbed out of his small cabin plane at the landing field and looked around for his chauffeur.

Spying him, coming running across the field for his luggage, he said to his pilot: "Great trip, Norton. Let me tell you, as man to man, you're the best pilot in the world. You know when to take a chance and when not to. If I can be half as good as you I'll be satisfied."

"Oh, I don't think I'm so good, Dr. Burns," Norton replied, with a pleased grin. "And you're coming on yourself. If your hair wasn't—the color it is——"

"Yes, my hair. It's got me into a lot of trouble in this life. Don't hesitate to call it red, Norton. . . . Hullo, Jimmy. . . . Everything all right at home?"

"Yes, sir." The chauffeur was grinning like the pilot. Both thought there was nobody like him— and they were right: there really wasn't anybody. "Glad to see you back, Dr. Burns."

"I'd be gladder to be back if Mrs. Burns and the family were there. Mail waiting, or did you bring it out?"

"I'm sorry I didn't, sir. I might have thought of that."

"You might, Jimmy—but if you get me home in fifteen minutes I'll excuse you. All right, here we go."

There they went, certainly. Striding across the field at a proper pace, jumping into the car, taking the wheel—as Jimmy had known he would, once he set foot in the slim, powerful roadster—there was no time lost.

It was fourteen minutes, exactly, when Red stood in the hall of his own home, sorting out the letters from Ellen, his wife, and Bob, his adopted son, away at a great boys' school. There was also a little note from the elder of his small daughters. All right. Fine news. Now, what was all the rest of this stuff? Riffling the pile through again he came upon one of those big, square, creamy-thick envelopes which usually mean just one thing—a wedding invitation. It looked innocent enough, as envelopes containing wedding invitations do; yet who can tell, upon curiously regarding the engraved formula within, what the conjunction of names may ultimately stand for? Usually nobody, no matter how many the prophets.

A previous wedding invitation, issued some dozen or so years before, had carried the names of Redfield Pepper Burns, M. D., and Ellen Beaumont Lessing. Red had met Ellen in his own town in the North, where she, a young widow from South Carolina, had been visiting friends next door to his office-home. He had had very little time to spend with her, patients, as always, obstructing any plans of his own that he might formulate. But he had somehow, between professional engagements, managed to attract her favorable attention, and had afterwards, when she had returned to her home, rushed South long enough to get a few hours of clear space in which to ask her to marry him.

She had had to come North again to do it, and even at the last minute the marriage had had to be delayed for three hours because of somebody's dire necessity. But the marriage vows, though contracted in such haste, had held—and had held tight.

Certain of Ellen's family, a branch of the Beaumonts, had been lured North by Ellen's change of residence and had been for some years settled within thirty miles of the Burnses. Among them was a young daughter upon whom Dr. Burns had been engaged to keep an eye and see that an earlier and critical illness should not prevent her growth into a strong womanhood. Both Red and Ellen were deeply fond of Sally Beaumont, had her over often for visits, and considered her very nearly their own property.

3

RED wasn't bothering just then about possible wedding invitations, and was about to cast the creamy thick envelope aside when the postmark caught his eye. It was that of the town where Sally Beaumont lived. He opened it in a hurry. He and Ellen hadn't been informed about this. Whom the deuce was Sally going to marry? It couldn't be . . .

His worst fears were confirmed. In spite of the times without number she had said she wouldn't marry Philip Filmore—Red disliked the very name —she was apparently about to do it. Engineered into it, of course, by her mother and her aunt, who were accustomed always to try to tell her what to do. It was curious about Sally, how she had let them manage her. Since she had become well and strong she had seemed upstanding enough, a modern girl, though never one of those assertive, boyish young persons who threw things around and told everybody what they thought. Sally had retained the fascinatingly yielding ways of her earlier Southern environment, and perhaps she had discovered them effective against the background of the comparatively new Northern influences and manners. But Sally was real, just the same, thought her uncle Red, and if she was going to marry Phil Filmore it was because somebody had made her think it ought to be done. Fools! If there was a thing in the world that ought not to be done, it was the tying together for better or worse—certain to be worse—of Sally Beaumont and that—that—well, it wouldn't be put into words, that was all, what Dr. Redfield Pepper Burns thought of young Filmore. But it was quite enough, and all of it unfavorable.

He picked up the thing again—he had tossed it to one side—to note the date of this intended, prepared for, and all-but-accomplished crime. With horror he discovered that it was—what was to-day? —the sixteenth—the seventeenth—one loses track of dates when absorbingly occupied—Sally was to be married on the nineteenth. . . . And this was —what frightful luck!—this was most certainly the eighteenth. And seven in the evening, at that. And he was thirty miles away. The rehearsal—yes, the actual rehearsal must be about to be staged—in the austere old white church on the village green which had seen many weddings. No time to be lost. Naturally, not a minute. And he wasn't accustomed to losing time.

4

STOPPING for nothing—Dr. Burns wasn't hungry now, anyway, though he had been ravenous when he came in—he called his car back. Within ten minutes he was on his way out, alone. In spite of the heavy traffic on a fine June evening, in forty-two minutes flat—he had cut into the line most recklessly all the way—the car pulled up in front of the lighted church, where it was perfectly evident that something was going on. For a moment Red's seasoned heart gave him a bad jolt. He couldn't have made a mistake—this wasn't the night of the wedding itself. No, of course not—only three motors stood in front, and no crowd had collected. It was the rehearsal, all right. Pretty late in the game: most people would consider the thing as good as done.

Red didn't consider it done, not by a long shot. He hadn't been doing emergency operations all these years for nothing. You could get in with your little old sharp knife—and other instruments—at almost the last minute, sometimes, and save a life. And he was, at this present almost last minute, quite ready to draw blood. The first incision!

He stole to the door, and to the shelter of one of the pillars which upheld the back gallery. There was the expected scene, with Ellen's sisters—Evelyn, Sally's mother, and Marian, her aunt—in charge. There were the bridesmaids—amazingly pretty girls—in gay summer evening wear. There were the ushers, in flannels—the best man, the maid of honor, the clergyman—everything as it was to be to-morrow night except the decorations, the clothes, and the solemnity. The bridal party were laughing through the rehearsal, considering the occasion one out of which they must get as much diversion as possible.

"Good Lord," thought Red grimly, "as well laugh over the rehearsal of a hanging." And scowled heavily, back under the shadow of the gallery, as he listened and watched.

"See here!" It was one of the ushers to another. "To save my life and what honor I may possess I can't keep step with that dirge. They've got to speed up the pace if they expect me to stop wobbling."

"You'll wobble anyway. You'll be lit—so'll we all. How else can we get through seeing this sort of thing to the finish?"

"Mrs. Beaumont—please!"—this was a bridesmaid—"do you really think we should carry our bouquets *that* way? *This* is how it was done at the Sipperleys, and everybody thought it was heaps more picturesque. Quainter—if you know what I mean."

"It makes no difference how it was done at the Sipperleys, Rosalie. I considered they looked very stiff held like that."

"Oh, very well." The speaker adjusted the position of the hymnal she was carrying—they were all carrying hymnals to illustrate the general slant of the bouquets of to-morrow night. She grinned at another bridesmaid and spoke under her breath. At the moment they were close to Red's pillar.

"Ever see such an old autocrat? She's planned every detail of this show. We and Sally haven't had a look-in."

"I know. It simply slays me to have to wear that peculiar shade of green. I feel like a young onion in it."

"I rather like it. But I detest and abominate the

hats. Neither big nor little—just neutral—terribly unbecoming!"

But Red had no ear for the chatter or the whispers. No eye for the bridesmaids or the ushers. He knew some of them—it was a gay set, that of Sally's. Through the Beaumonts he had been called to certain of their friends' families. The life of one girl present he had saved for her by a hair—it was the one who didn't like to wear green. But he didn't think of these things, he was intensely concentrated on Sally. He hadn't yet got a real look at her face, but he was watching her back. Such a little thing, was Sally, though no baby in years—she must be all of twenty-five, he knew. But there seemed a sort of listlessness about even that back of hers—sun tanned, after the fashion—sturdy enough—or it had been sturdy, thanks to his care of her, when he saw it last. Was it perceptibly thinner now, or was that his imagination?

Finally, he got a glimpse of her face. She had been obeying orders automatically, pacing down the aisle beside her older brother—her father had been dead for two years.—What a lot of weight young Horace Beaumont had put on, by the way! His neck was thick—far too thick, Red knew, for his age.—Suddenly her aunt Marian called to Sally, and she turned, and Red saw her face.

The sight of it quickened his purpose—doubled his purpose. Sally, though she smiled, though she looked as adorable as ever, wasn't happy. Why, couldn't they all see that? What were they doing, her mother and aunt and brother, putting her through her paces, making a background of themselves for this impossible union? There was Philip Filmore, the man she was to marry, ogling the bridesmaids, as he had ogled every pretty girl since he left the nursery. They were treating him as they always treated him, playing up to him. Careless, handsome, obviously carrying as much liquor as he could hold and still stand firmly on his feet, he was paying Sally only the most casual attention. He was no good—he had never been any good, Red said fiercely to himself. And he wasn't going to marry Sally. If she looked like that to-night, how would she look to-morrow night? He tried to imagine it, and shut his eyes tight together for an instant, while the wiry curly red hair on his head might have stiffened and stood straight up, like a dog's hackles, if a man's hair could act that way. It *felt* that way, to Red; he could feel it stiffening.

5

THE rehearsal was over at last. The hymnals were shoved back into the racks without regard to where they might belong. The group strolled up the aisle, in detached twos and threes, chattering. Red had withdrawn still farther into the shadow where nobody could notice him. He wanted to hear and see everything possible before determining exactly what to do.

The thing that struck him as extraordinary was that during that passage up the aisle Sally seemed to be quite alone. In the midst of many, and although she had always been the object of much attention, she was none the less companioned by nobody in particular to-night, least of all by Phil himself. He was laughing into the black eyes of the prettiest and most striking looking bridesmaid, lighting a cigarette even while still here in the church, and whispering something into the girl's ear to which she responded with such a look as meant but one thing to Red, as he caught it—her preoccupation with the bridegroom to the exclusion of all others present. . . . After all, it might mean

little, said this keen-eyed spy to himself. He understood that all young people in these days played at
love making as a matter of course, and insisted, if
you charged them with it, that it stood for nothing
at all, and you were an old fool if you attempted
to check up on anybody just because he or she played
the part. Just the same, Red resented seeing Sally
left to herself even for the two minutes that it took
for them all to get out of the church—she, by far,
in his eyes, the sweetest child that ever——

As he followed them out it seemed to be the
same outside. Yet Sally wasn't appearing to mind
it. She turned a little aside from the party and
stood looking off over the village green to the left,
where there were no houses, only a vista through
the trees in the old burying ground at the side of
the church toward a high hill, with the summer
stars shining above it. She too seemed preoccupied
—but with no man. Her slight figure in its floating
evening draperies, lighted only by a distant arc
light in the centre of the green, made a wistful outline against the darkness over there.

Red came up to her and spoke gently: "Sally—
want to see me?"

She turned quickly, stared at him for a minute,

then gave him both hands—icy cold they were, as he instantly noticed. "Oh, Uncle *Red!*"

There was a strange note in her voice—it fitted with what he had already observed of her. Yet she smiled dazzlingly at him, in her own captivating way, her face lighting, as it always had at his approach.

"Just got back from a three-weeks' absence and found the invitation. Dashed up here to see you—couldn't wait till to-morrow."

"No! How wonderful of you! Is Aunt Ellen here too?"

"She's away—back next week. Knows nothing of this. Somebody must have slipped up on forwarding."

Sally's mother, Evelyn Beaumont, caught sight of them and came up to them hurriedly. Sally's Aunt Marian followed. They greeted him with gracious warmth.

"My dear Red! Where have you been? It seemed so strange we hadn't heard from Ellen and you. Have you been away?"

He explained again. By this time the whole group had observed the newcomer. As has been said, some of them knew him well. The bridesmaid who didn't like her green frock fluttered over to him, some of the others following. Philip Filmore was not one of the number, nor was the girl who was still beside him, though they looked on intently.

"Why, Dr. Burns! Of course Sally couldn't have got married without you and your perfectly fascinating wife."

"You do take time for weddings, don't you, you busy man?"

"Come." Mrs. Beaumont spoke to the group. "This rehearsal has taken much more time than we planned for, and a little supper is waiting for you over at the house. Come, Dr. Burns, Sally— all of you. It will be lovely walking across the green —it will refresh us all."

"If you don't mind, Evelyn, I'm going to take Sally off in my car for an hour." Red's mind was fully made up now, as to his course. The sight of Sally's face at close range, in the instant before she had had time to summon that gallant smile, had shocked him. He didn't care what he did or whom he offended. No time for feeling his way, he must get Sally to himself at once and find out what that look meant.

"Why, Dr. Burns!" This was Sally's Aunt

Marian, who had never quite accepted her sister Ellen's marrying the blunt surgeon from the North.

"She can't be spared now," Sally's mother said. "This is the very last evening she can spend with her bridal party before she's married."

"That's obvious, and I'm sorry, but it's no real reason why I shouldn't see Sally. If I know the custom, you've all been putting over parties for the last three weeks in Sally's honor. They've undoubtedly been very jolly, but the girl's tired out. I'll freshen her up with a good slow drive with an elderly uncle who'll let her relax. Jump in, Sally."

"Sally!" Her mother spoke in her ear. "This is really——"

"Just for a few minutes, Mother? We won't be gone any time at all."

"Oh, let her go!" This was Phil Filmore himself, lounging up, one hand in his pocket. "How are you, sir? Nice of you to get back for the wedding."

"Was it?" Red forced himself to shake hands with young Filmore—there was no way out of that. Nobody could know that it was the handshake before the fight. Phil himself might have sensed opposition stiffening the blunt surgeon's manner; but what of that? What use to oppose a marriage the rehearsal for which had just taken place? There had been a time, a year ago, when Dr. Burns, in his own office, had said some pretty straight things to young Filmore, who had recently undergone a minor operation which might later have been a major one. Neither had forgotten the trend the parting interview had taken. Distaste had tinctured Burns's gruff advice.

"Go on as you're going, and the first real crisis that hits you will send you under. Don't you *want* to have enough physical resistance, by way of a clean blood stream, to live your life with? You can't get it by your damnable methods."

"*You* seem to have weathered the storms of youth, sir," had been Filmore's retort. He had left the office on the words. It would hardly have been safe to stay longer.

To-night, secure in his position, Filmore even closed Red's car door after getting Sally's delicate skirts out of the way. He made an urbane gesture of farewell, accompanied by speech not so urbane:

"Hit it up with him, Sally—it's your last chance before the shackles go on. Let me remind you,

Dr. Burns, there's a bad detour just beyond the West Egerton crossroads. Don't feel it necessary to get back for the end of the party—the bridesmaids will dance with the deserted bridegroom. Or —I may run off with one of them. Justifiable, in the circumstances, eh?"

The speech highly amused the bridal party, but it didn't amuse Sally's mother and aunt. As for Red, he made no reply. He edged his motor through the group of laughing young people, who threatened by blocking the car to stop it. One girl pulled off a slipper and held it up, gleaming in the light from the church door, her arm across the shoulder of an usher for support.

"Shall I throw it after them?" she cried.

The best man caught at a silver ribbon which girdled the slightly heavy figure of the maid of honor. He would have pulled it off if she hadn't screamed and held on to it.

"Wanted to tie it to the back bumper," he complained. "Couldn't you be a sport?"

Sally's mother and her aunt had turned their backs on the scene, annoyed to the core with this interfering brother-in-law.

"Exactly like him," complained Marian bitterly

"I've always said he can be the worst barbarian——"

"It's precisely why I didn't write him of the engagement." Evelyn, Sally's mother, was white under her skillfully applied rouge and powder. "Nobody ever knows what he'll do. Rushing the child off, away from everybody, when she's worn out as she is. I thought she just couldn't stand up for the rehearsal, when we came to the church."

"Still, perhaps she'll really rest a little, in the night air. I do hope Redfield will have sense enough to bring her back in ten minutes."

"Rest! Did anybody ever rest with Redfield Burns? You might as well try to rest with a steel riveter under your window."

In spite of this characterization—which might be, in a way, not a bad one at times—Red, with Sally, was at the moment already a half mile away from all these people, as quiet as a sleeping dog. But with one eye open and all his senses alert. Sally had snuggled down into the deep seat, laid her head back, and was staring up at the stars. Red never used a closed car when he could help it: in summer, at least—unless rain were pouring, the top was always down, as to-night.

6

PRESENTLY he heard a smothered breath drawn. He had expected it. But he still maintained his silence. Give her a little more time to rest, before he should come at her.

Meanwhile, his mind was busy analyzing the probable reasons why Sally's mother had been so anxious to bring about this marriage. The first one was easy; it had ever been the mainspring of most mothers' ambitions for their daughters. The Filmores were socially more prominent and far richer than the Beaumonts in the Northern village where the Filmores lived half the year, the Beaumonts the whole of it. The Southern family had had its own unimpeachable position in the South, but the head of the family was gone, and finances were comparatively low. And to Evelyn Beaumont, who as a young beauty had married at eighteen, her daughter Sally was at twenty-five "getting on" and should be led to the altar without more delay. Sally's own indifference to the subject would only spur Evelyn on.

Yes, these reasons were obvious, and probably

foremost. But Red's training and observation presented him with a subtler explanation—one of which Evelyn herself was probably unconscious. To her, married so early, still exceedingly attractive, widowed for two years, this young man, Philip Filmore, with his good looks—Red supposed women thought him good-looking—*he* didn't—his easy, flattering manners toward them, his probably endearing attentions to the mother while he was visiting the house to see the daughter—all this had been to Evelyn a sort of renewal of her own days of romance, hardly over for a woman of her type. It was really she who was in love with Phil and with the idea of bringing him into her own life to stay. That was it, and all modern examination of the motives which underlie the more obscure relations between men and women supported Red's recognition of it. In a curious way, he said to himself, it was not Sally but Evelyn who was getting married, obnoxious as the thought might be. All the more reason, then—and a big reason too—why it shouldn't be allowed.

Red turned to look at the still figure beside him, an infinite pity in his heart. Could he tell Sally anything of all this? Hardly, unless it should become really necessary.

Finally she spoke. "Uncle Red, why in the world did you do this?"

"Because you were tired out and needed it. Isn't that right?"

"I am a little tired," she admitted.

"But perfectly happy, of course."

"Why not? Why should you think anything else? If you knew how all the parties one has to go through with take it out of a bride, you wouldn't wonder I'm not bubbling to-night."

"The rest were bubbling. They've been through 'em all with you, haven't they?"

"Yes, but——"

"But——?"

Sally turned on him with spirit. "Uncle Red, you seem to think—I don't know what you think."

"Yes, I think it. That you're not happy."

"Are brides—ever? All I've ever seen at the last minute have been scared or doubtful—or something. They're all tired and excited. And thinking about it —well—it's—quite a change. Suddenly—one's freedom is gone."

"It is. Still—if she really loves him a lot——"

There was a long silence again. Then Sally said in a strained voice: "I don't believe I quite knew how really sleepy and lazy I am. Just being off here with you in the stillness makes me—it almost makes me wish we could just go on and on—and not get back till everybody had gone and the lights were out. Isn't that absurd? And of course I don't mean it. I'll be all right in the morning."

"Are you sure?"

"Why, of course."

"I mean—*sure?* And all right forever after?"

There was no answer, except that Sally drew herself up from her half-reclining position against the car's easy cushioning and sat erect. There was a proud lift of her head now, which Red could easily note in the semi-darkness of the June night.

He looked for a crossroad he knew of, found it, turned up it. It was a narrow unpaved road and led up over a hill. At the top of that hill, with nobody in sight or likely to appear, he stopped the car and sat silently looking at the beautiful young profile beside him. Finally Sally turned her head, and he could see her trying to scan his face in turn.

"Well?" he suggested gently. "Is this a time for anything but the absolute truth, my dear? There seems to be nobody but me to urge it. Even you are trying to lie as gallantly as though I were a spy and you intending to die in defense of your country rather than give me one notion as to the whereabouts of the secret maps and orders. Don't you trust me, Sally, after all this time?"

"Of course I trust you. But—Uncle Red—*what's the use?*"

It gave her away, that one smothered phrase. He pressed his advantage quickly.

"Sally, you don't want to marry the man you're all set to marry? Answer me honestly, for your life."

It was the way he spoke to patients when he knew they were holding back something. Not harshly, but with his will behind it, reinforcing their weaker wills. They always told him what he needed to know.

He could feel her quickened breathing, knew that she controlled herself with a supreme effort. He waited patiently; he knew his power, and he didn't hesitate to exercise it, because he must save her.

Finally she said under her breath: "I don't want to marry him, Uncle Red. But I meant nobody to even guess—least of all you."

"Most of all me, because I can do something about it."

"No—it's too late. I knew you and Aunt Len didn't like him. But somehow—he had a way—at times. . . . And I hadn't cared for any of the others. . . . Mother——" But on that she stopped quickly.

He knew. Yes, Mother. . . . But he didn't say it. Instead he had a quick question that startled her into answering it as instantly as he put it.

"This is the next thing I want to know, Sally. Please tell me this: Is there somebody else you'd marry instead, if you could?"

"There was. He's married."

"How long ago?"

"Four years."

"Is he one of your set, here, so that you have to look at him?"

"No. He's a long way off. I've hardly ever seen him since I went to his wedding. He's never thought of me, Uncle Red. I just worshiped him like a silly schoolgirl—as I was. I'm not thinking about him now—really I'm not. But I suppose once knowing him has made all the others seem—well—neutral."

"I see," said Red Pepper. He lighted a cigarette and smoked a third of it before he said anything more. Finally: "Well, I think he's out of the picture.

Just a Sir Galahad or—to be more modern—an aviation hero, or somebody of that sort—capturing your imagination without his having broken any lances for you—or crumpled any wings."

"That's all," admitted Sally, with another deep sigh. "Yes, that's all. The quite impossible dream. But he doesn't exist for me. So I might as well marry Phil—as I'm doing to-morrow night. It doesn't matter." The next minute she crumpled up in her place and was sobbing helplessly against Red's arm. "Oh," she gasped, "oh, God—it does matter. It matters horribly!"

"Then," said Red, very firmly indeed, "you're not going to do it." His hand came around and patted her silky dark head. "You're not going to do it, do you hear, Sally Beaumont?"

She became suddenly breathless with attention, her sobbing ceasing. "What do you mean? Oh, what do you mean?"

"Why—just that. If you feel that way about it, you're not going to do it."

"There's no way to stop it."

It was a cry of despair, and it shook him. But his manner changed.

He removed her from his arm, made her sit up

straight, sat up straight beside her, took her hand in his with a firm grip.

"There's a way to stop *anything*. Of course, it's your mother and Marian who've been putting this through. The Lord only knows why you've let them. But it's not too late. All there's going to be of this ghastly marriage is the rehearsal for it. We're going back to tell Filmore we're not going through with it. Then we'll tackle the job of breaking it to your mother and aunt."

"Oh—how *can* I!"

"How *can't* you! Marry a man you don't even like and who—listen to me, Sally—didn't act to me to-night—I was watching that rehearsal—as though you meant a hang more to him than he does to you. One of those bridesmaids——"

"Yes, I know." Sally stiffened, and an edge came into her voice—an edge Red was glad to hear. "Dorothea Morton. She's mad about him."

"I should say he was at least willing to have her mad about him. In my opinion he's such a damned prodigal he's spoiled his chance of ever being honestly in love with any girl. Tell me—do you think he's going to suffer over losing you?"

"Only his pride. And of course my pride would suffer too. We'd be in all the papers."

"Better be in the papers now for a broken engagement than a year from now for a broken marriage. Come, my dear—show me the good backbone you've got—not this rubbery imitation one that's been soaked in something that's taken the lime out of it. . . . See here—do you hate to send back the wedding presents?" His hazel eyes gleamed. "Hate to let 'em go, eh?"

"No!" Sally's tone was violent. "I hate the sight of them. I've hated every one that came."

"Then let's make a dash back to the house and get it over." He set his foot on the starter. She put her hand on his arm.

"Uncle Red," she said in a stifled voice, "do you really think I'm justified? What—what—can I say to Phil?"

"The truth—that's all. Want me to put the words into your mouth?"

"Oh, no!—Or—yes—yes—I do. I'm as frightened as that."

"Then suppose we face him together. I know what's the matter with you now, Sally. You showed a lot of pluck in pulling out of that little pussy-cat adolescence of yours and fighting to get strong. But you've got all tangled up in this thing, and it's made

you lose something I was sure you'd gained. It's the
deuce of a thing to lose, and I don't know where you
lost it, but you've got to get it back. This experience'll help you do it. *It's the power to make a decision for yourself and to stand to it. Or—to reverse
it with equal firmness when you see it was the wrong
decision, and to stand to that reversal.* I don't know
which is the more important—I guess they go together. I've had to do it many a time, Sally. On the
operating table. Getting in and finding the thing I
didn't expect to find. Changing all my plans on the
instant. Trying to save a life that way instead of the
other. Suppose I'd felt I wasn't justified in making
the change? I've known a man to operate on the
organ he'd announced was involved—but wasn't—
just to save his face, and then go on and do the other
thing, pretending he'd known all the time that both
lesions were there."

"But this isn't surgery we're talking of. It's—so
different!"

"I'll say it'll be surgery when we've done it," announced Red grimly. "Amputating everybody's
pride. Pride! What a lot of mistakes have been
made because of it. Well, here we go. Just about
cover it before the party disperses, won't we? It's

got to be done to-night. The sun mustn't rise on any more wedding gifts being opened; it's a lot of trouble to do 'em up again."

7

THEY did face Philip Filmore together. They had to take him away from Dorothea Morton to do it, for he was sitting on the step below her with his head on her lap and her fingers in his hair. The whole group were in the moonlight on the pillared rear porch of the Beaumont home. The others were much amused, indeed quite thrilled, when Dr. Burns and Sally Beaumont came suddenly out upon them. They all looked at Phil Filmore and Dorry Morton, expecting an instant change of attitude. Or no—of course, it was much cannier for the pair to handle the situation the way they did handle it between them.

"Thankful you've got back, Sally," murmured Dorothea. "I'm stiff in the joints from keeping up this pose for you to see if you ever did come back from your elopement. Phil planned it to be much more effective than this, but he got so sleepy."

Phil hardly stirred. His handsome head moved slightly on his companion's silken knees, and his eyes opened, glancing up at Sally, through mere slits in his heavily lashed lids. He reached for a cigarette, lighted it lazily, and spoke into the silence.

"Just having my last bachelor fling, Sally. The next time I put my head on a girl's lap I'll be a married man—and maybe it'll be even more fun, eh?"

Dr. Burns answered him. Red's blood was boiling. "Filmore, when you're thoroughly awake, may I see you in the library? And will the rest of you wait, please?"

Filmore rose slowly, swaying a little on his slender legs. He drew in heavily on the cigarette, blew two long straight columns of smoke from his nostrils, let the rest drift from his slightly opened lips, tossed the cigarette, still alight, upon the lawn, and came toward Dr. Burns and Sally.

"It almost looks as though you two had something on your minds," he said pleasantly. "Let's find out what it is." He glanced back at Dorothea. "Who knows?" he murmured. And followed the others in.

In ten minutes it was over, in the library, in the subdued light from a Persian lamp.

"I'm not going to marry you, Phil," said Sally, so bravely that Red was proud of her. "I'm sorry I ever promised to. It wasn't fair to either of us. I didn't love you. It's dreadful to have let it go on till the last minute, but I've decided it's better to stop it even now than to go through with it. I don't imagine you'll care."

There was a long minute's silence, while Filmore regarded his bride elect with astonished eyes. Then he made her a quick, stiffly formal bow.

"Just as you say, my dear Sally," he said. "Dorothea and I've rather been hoping for this, but we'd about given up. When you went off with your jolly uncle, hope revived a bit. He's the sort who doesn't hesitate to say what he thinks. What he thinks is immaterial to me, but what you think goes a long way. If you think you don't want to marry me—that settles it. It seems a pity to send all those gorgeous presents back—but perhaps the givers'll just store 'em for a little and then send 'em to Dorry."

Sally took a step towards him.

"Do you imagine you love Dorothea, Phil?" she asked.

"Why not? She's a wonder."

"Did you ever think you loved me?"

"Well—" he was lighting another cigarette— "you did attract me, for a time, my dear. But—I seemed to get over it. Getting out of it was another matter. The Filmores don't do that."

"Don't they!" This was Dr. Red, and he suddenly towered over the younger and slighter man. "One of them has got out of it by his own methods —singular ones, as they seem to me. Not that I don't rejoice to see you out of it, but I'd like to have seen you do it through the door. Just one door—the truth—as Sally herself has walked through it now."

"Oh?" inquired Philip Filmore. Then he lost grip of himself, his voice became rough, his manner sneering. "Since you've taken a hand, sir, I'll look to you to see this mess through. You and Sally. It's up to you to face 'em all. You won't mind the people on the porch, there. They'll get an awful kick out of it. But when it comes to Mrs. Beaumont—and her sister—I think you're going to have the time of your life. As for me—I'll be driving Dorothea home. We'll miss the show. Too bad—I rather hate to miss it, too."

Red put his hand under Sally's arm and turned her toward the door. Neither of them gave Phil another look.

8

THE telling of the group on the porch didn't take long. Dr. Burns made a dignified announcement, his arm still in Sally's, whose face was very white. Except for a low murmur here and there, the news was received in a shocked silence. One smothered, hysterical giggle came from the girl who sat nearest Dorothea. As for Phil, he wasn't there at all. He had remained inside, looking out from an unlighted room. What was to be said by him or by anybody else, Red and Sally didn't stay to hear. They went back into the house, around and up by the curving staircase, to find the two whom they most dreaded to face. Even the redoubtable surgeon dreaded it, and had the grace to feel pretty sorry for his sisters-in-law, really charming women in ordinary times.

There was just one speech of his which remained in Sally's memory after it was all over:

"Evelyn, no matter how hard on you this whole break-up is—and I appreciate that it can't help being that—there's just one thing to remember: You wouldn't hesitate at any measures necessary to save your daughter's life. Measures to save her happiness are hard for you to adopt at the eleventh hour, but there's nothing else to do. I'd run away with her myself and never come back rather than see her make this marriage."

Tears, hysteria—they were to be expected.

Nerves worn with weeks of planning and executing, with visits to dressmakers, with the whole machinery of an elaborate wedding. There really was, even to the blunt doctor, every reason why Sally's mother should go all to pieces. But nothing could justify, to him, her wild reproaches of Sally, her fury over the breaking off of this match, which seemed to her to be so eminently desirable——

But Sally rose to it. "I'm terribly sorry, Mother," she said, her eyes pitiful but her lips controlling themselves. "It's all—*all*—my fault—absolutely my fault. I should never have let it happen. I was weak. I knew it shouldn't. Forgive me—if you can. But anyhow, you do want me to be happy, don't you, dear?"

Mrs. Beaumont raised her tear-stained face. "Happy!" she cried. "Do you mean to tell me you're happy, after having done this crazy thing? . . . Don't you care a particle for having hurt poor dear Phil like this—to say nothing of the rest of us?"

"Phil wants to marry Dorothea," said Sally. Then she added steadily: "And as for my being happy— right now—of course I'm not. I feel a fiend to have upset everybody like this. And yet—compared with the way I felt an hour ago—I'm so happy I could cry for joy."

"Come away before you do it," said Red in her ear. Then he added: "I'm going to take Sally off for a few days, Evelyn. You'll do better here without her. Good-night, my dear. I haven't meant to be a brute—but a man has to be, sometimes, to save women from throwing themselves over a cliff into the sea."

Sally packed a bag blindly, not knowing what she put into it except that she made sure of a few necessaries. It *was* better to go, she knew, even though it meant leaving everything to her mother and aunt. The repacking and dispatching of the wedding gifts would be done, as it would have been done, in any case, by men hired for such business. But with herself out of the way it would be easier for her mother to give it all up, to let down from tension, and to come back to normal. One thing was certain: Mrs. Beaumont wouldn't have any disconsolate bridegroom to condole with. Phil wouldn't come near her. And as for his family, well, Sally couldn't help them. The thing was done.

9

SALLY and Dr. Burns drove the thirty miles in almost absolute silence. It was impossible for her to talk;

her excitement had been replaced by something close
to a sort of spiritual collapse. She had become numb
to feeling, she thought, and welcomed the release
from any need to bother her tired brain. The com-
forting nearness of the silent man beside her, the
knowledge that he would expect nothing more of
her to-night, but would understand just how limp
she had become, was of itself soothing. The warm
air of the quiet night lapped her as with a gently
flowing river. She needn't do one thing, smile one
smile, say one word, she didn't want to. After weeks
of what she looked back on as pretense, acting in a
drama whose ending she was dreading with every
hour it drew nearer, she was like one who sees the
audience vanish, the lights extinguished, and the
need for further effort gone. Bed—rest—sleep—
these seemed the only things in the world she
wanted, at the end of the drive. Let the coming day
take care of itself. In the home of Aunt Ellen and
Uncle Red it could do just that.

As he drove like a meteor through the night,
Red's thoughts were again busy. Having disposed of
one problem, he was mentally attacking another.

"When did that letter come?" he was asking himself. "And what the devil did I do with it? Worse

yet, what did I do with the layout he sent? Anything may have happened while I was away. If I can't find those . . . See here—I've got to find 'em. They're essential. If I weren't so infernally careless with stuff that's sent me . . ."

He worried about it all the way home. A letter. A lot of material mailed "under separate cover." Remembering all this had been a magnificent inspiration which had come to him at the time that he was waiting outside the Beaumont house while Sally made ready to accompany him. But it was no inspiration if he couldn't remember where to find that which had caused it.

"Should have a file case for such things just as much as for patients' histories. Invaluable sometimes. If I *can't* find 'em . . ."

He grew foggier and foggier over it. A fellow could be clever enough at one hour and just plain moron the next. He became positive that he had, as the law says, destroyed the evidence. When he took Sally into his own home, at last, his one idea was to begin his search the very moment he was free, and keep it up the rest of the night, if need be.

"In here," said Red, indicating a small but inviting guest room and following Sally in to set down her little handbag on the rack meant for it. She had often slept there before, but the place had never seemed such a refuge as to-night. "And I want you to stay here till you are ready to get up. Pop into a hot bath—it'll help let you down. In fifteen minutes I'll come in and feel your pulse and tuck you in."

She obeyed him literally, and when she lay, a slim, quiet figure, between Aunt Ellen's fine, faintly fragrant sheets, she let both bare arms fall straight out, to right and left of her, closed her eyes, and lay waiting for Red to keep his promise. That meant as much as anything just now.

"All right?" He came softly in, bearing a little tray with a glass of hot milk upon it, and some thin, crisp wafers. Sally had switched off her lights, but those in the hall outside showed her clearly to him. Her eyes were open now and regarding him.

"Yes—quite all right," she whispered.

"Sit up a minute and drink this. I suppose you've been living on fussy food for weeks. This will make you think you're a small girl again, and make you sleep, too."

She sat up, and he placed himself upon the edge

of the bed behind her, so that his shoulder supported her. She leaned against it comfortably as she drank. Oh, there never was anybody like Uncle Red, who could put her through the fight she'd been in to-night, egging her on, standing by her—and then treating her like the exhausted child she had turned into. She took as long as she could to drink the milk and nibble the wafers, so that she might feel his warm heart beating against her back. Why couldn't all women be as lucky as Aunt Ellen and find for themselves men like this, instead of marrying gay blades of no account who would never become towers of strength like Redfield Burns, but would keep their wives uncertain of them all their days? The picture of Phil Filmore and Dorothea Morton came suddenly before her. If Dorry actually should marry Phil, she would have to look at pictures such as Sally had seen to-night until she became hardened to them and ceased to mind that she had an incorrigible philanderer for a husband. Or—Dorry would doubtless keep up her end, matching or outdoing Phil. Then there would be a divorce—of course. That was the way that divorces mostly came, wasn't it?

"Now lie down, child," said Red in her ear. "Stop thinking about all that. Just remember you're here

—and safe—and that this isn't the end of your life. It's only the beginning. I promise you that."

He laid her down himself and drew the sheet to her breast. How many times, during these past years, when he had been trying to build up her physical strength, had she looked up into his sturdy face, promised him she would do exactly as he asked her, no matter how disagreeable his orders, and been rewarded his smile and his big bear hug? She put up her arms now, as she had done then, and felt again —it had been a long time now since this had happened, because Red's prescriptions had worked out so well—his arms about her, his cheek pressed against hers. He held her very close to-night, with a fierce sort of pressure, as though having rescued her he was telling her again that she was safe.

"Good-night, Uncle Red. You're such a darling."

"You're pretty much of one yourself, Sally."

He went out and closed the door, and though she wouldn't have thought it possible, because she had been sleeping very badly ever since those wedding invitations had gone out, she was off almost instantly, like the tired swimmer who has at last touched bottom and has waded up to the dry sand and thrown himself down upon it.

10

ALONE in his own room Red went to his desk and
began his search. That letter—that big manilla envelope containing a set of photographs—what on
earth had he done with them? The letter presently
came to light, but it took him a long time to un-
earth the rest of his material. Finally he discovered
it, in a many-shelved cupboard where he was accustomed to fire things when he was in a hurry to clear
the desk. All right! Now to make big medicine for
Sally, if strategy would do it.

He reread the letter, which had come from the
wilds of the Canadian Northwest. He was much
interested in that letter.

DEAR DR. BURNS:

You certainly knew what you were doing when
you sent me off here. It's been a great job, growing
steadily more interesting, and I never can tell you
what I've got out of it. When I came I didn't begin
to know how soft I was, nor in how much danger of
never amounting to anything. But physically I've
grown hard as nails, working on this great piece of

construction. I'd never have believed I'd get such an amazing kick out of my little part in the whole thing. I hope I'm of a bit better stuff mentally, too —or wherever it is that a fellow begins to grow something besides pin-feathers.

It was the most magnificent luck that I could be under the Englishman, Leslie Warden, you knew and liked so much. He's been a regular trainer for me, both for the engineering job and for the much bigger job of life. I've had more out of him than I ever got out of the schools. Most unassuming fellow in the world, as you know, but the real thing is in him—the thing one has to learn to live by. You know what that is, Dr. Burns, I don't need to try to tell you. I couldn't put it into words, anyway.

In another month, I'm coming home. Now that the two years are over, during which time I haven't been out of the wilderness for more than a day at a time, I'm getting a tremendous thrill out of the thought that in four or five weeks more I'll be back in the States. During all that time I've hardly been out of high boots, so to speak. And seeing only men. Most of them pretty rough, but I've learned how to get on with them, and a few of them have been corking. And always there was Warden!

I keep having a funny recollection of an hour during Commencement week, just before I left, when I was walking across the campus, on a wonderful June night, with a pretty girl—an awfully pretty girl—with whom I'd been dancing, and of wondering why I was bored to death. I know how foolish that sounds! I thought I was tired of girls, tired of everything, was on my way to making a failure of life. I was booked for this job, but that seemed to me just a way of escape, for a while, from my world. I didn't expect to like it. I hadn't taken any honors of any sort; you know I'd just barely squeaked through. I hadn't even been especially popular. Four years before, I'd seen my brother Rivers walk away with everything. He's still taking honors, by the way, and always will be, and I'm darned proud of him. As for me, I'm only just getting fit to take anything—the next job, probably. But, Dr. Burns . . .

Well, maybe you know how a fellow feels, after such an absence, at the thought of meeting girls and women again. I expect I'll be scared to death of them—forgotten my manners and how to talk to them, if I ever knew. But I want to meet some. I might better say I want to meet some *one*. For I'm going to be off again in only two months with Leslie

Warden, and this time we won't be quite so iso-lated. He may be getting married in the interval, and if he should, he feels it will be safe to bring his wife. If she isn't game to come that will end it, for he thinks his life for years will be on these out-of-civilization jobs. If she does come, I suppose I'll envy him.

Dr. Burns, you're the greatest doctor and the wisest man I know. When I get home I'll be thrown with plenty of girls—my family will see to that. It will be the old story, and I'll be bewildered among them, and a good bit shy, as I always was. The kind of girls I'll meet won't be the kind I'm thinking of. If you happened to know of anybody I could meet right away . . . You see, I've only those two months, with another two years in the wilds to fol-low, and I could waste every minute of the time just playing around. I can't afford to do that. And a fel-low on a job in the mountains and valleys where bridges and dams are built has a chance to be pretty lonesome when it comes to moonlight nights of a sort that get in a quite different sort of work on him than—well—than that which makes him leery of cocktails and dance music at home, lest he make a fool of himself with the wrong girl.

But that's enough of that, and more than likely you're smiling over this naïve, schoolboy sort of maundering. No, I know you're not smiling—except in an understanding sort of way. And I wouldn't write a word of it to another soul I know.

Anyhow, whether you can prescribe for me in this way, as you prescribed so successfully two years ago when I came into your office looking like a piece of suet, or whether I'm suggesting the impossible, I'm coming straight to your office again when I get back. I want to see you, and I hope you'll be glad to see me. I'm sending under separate cover some photographs of the great bridge, with a couple of close ups of Leslie and myself. I'll admit I was glad to have them, to show people what Leslie Warden is like. Even so, nobody who doesn't know him can guess.

The letter was signed "Jefferson Shipley." As Burns studied the pictures of his young friend Jeff and the Englishman, Warden, an expression of intense satisfaction spread over his face. Jeff looked every inch a man, and no less a gentleman—he had always been that—for the rough clothing and the wind blowing his hair.

Red's thoughts went back to Sally Beaumont; his mind had been working on this possibility for her ever since he had suddenly remembered Jeff's letter. It now occurred to him with some force that Jeff's elder brother Rivers might very conceivably be the man to whom Sally had referred as having captured her youthful admiration and whom she thought she couldn't forget. Jeff himself she might never have known, except as a youngster, only a little older than herself; while she, in those years of growing up, had thought nothing of him, only of his brother, who had been such a shining mark for general approval, not to mention that of the girls in their twenties, one of whom he had married. If it should be so . . .

Burns whistled softly to himself. And even if it shouldn't, here was Jeff, begging him to introduce him to the right girl, because he had so little time to find her before he should again plunge into work in remote places. Well, was Sally the right girl? Was she equal to the order of being a wife for such a man as Jeff had become? Red rather thought, in view of all he had known of her in past years, that she was capable of becoming such a wife. He still didn't understand how she had ever thought she could marry Phil Filmore, yet—well—hadn't he himself, in his earlier days, done many a mad thing which he had afterwards regretted? Why should he think an exquisite little beauty like Sally ought to have been wiser than her clever but unwise mother?

If she could know Jeff, it might be the making of her. And she was, Red would swear it, the sort of girl with whom Jeff could not only look at moonlight in a canyon and be glad that she was there, but be glad next day that she was with him, when the moonlight was gone and the sun was shining or the rain raining on the less exalted business of every day. In any case, he didn't hesitate for a moment to undertake the business of bringing them together, though he fully recognized that it couldn't be done by means of a bludgeon.

"No, not by a bludgeon," said he to himself, "though I'm afraid that represents my usual style of finesse. I must be more artful than that. Let's see. . . ."

II

HE LOOKED about him for a frame into which to put the photograph he liked best. It was rather a large one, made like the others in the set by a photographer who was getting together material for a magazine article on this great piece of engineering construction of which Jeff's friend, the Englishman, Leslie Warden, was one of the assistant engineers. Red's eye lighting on a picture on his wall which contained a mere landscape in France some patient had sent him, he quite ruthlessly took out his knife, ripped away the backing, clawed out the small nails, and removed that picture, beautiful enough of itself, but lacking the human element which was Red's first interest, always. The power in a personality—that was what he sought, before everything else.

Jefferson Shipley and Leslie Warden, standing, two slim sinewy figures against the sky line, presently looked at Dr. Burns out of the appropriate setting of a simple black frame. Next, to place it where it would catch the eye! Just above his desk was the spot, at the left, where anyone interviewing him would be sure to see it. He removed another picture from the wall; it was that of a distinguished English surgeon, but he went into the discard for the time being, just the same. Burns stood back, hands in pockets, eyeing the result. There was a wicked sparkle in his eye. The trap was set. It wouldn't be his fault if Sally Beaumont, though fresh from pacing down the aisle in rehearsal for a wedding which would never come off, should within a day or two in the house notice the photograph and ask for the story thereof.

Red thought he could tell that story—with the necessary reservations. As he remembered seeing Rivers Shipley the last time, perhaps a year ago, he was still the charmingly urbane and interesting person who had been a leader all through the schools and was now doing unusually creditable work in the world. But there was little question in Red's mind that the photograph of Jefferson Shipley, in his rough engineer's garb, in his face a strong resemblance to his elder brother, could be a formidable rival to any girlish memories of that engagingly picturesque figure. Jeff might not be quite so picturesque, but Red had an idea that he had the real stuff in him, and more than likely to an even greater degree than Rivers, who had "taken all the honors."

As he left the room finally for bed he gave the photograph one more glance before he switched off the lights. The trap was set, he said to himself with a grin, if it wasn't sprung. It wouldn't be his fault if some day—*snap!*

If that happened it would, in his opinion, be a case of justifiable homicide.

LETTER from Dr. Burns to his sister, Anne Sutherland, in a sanitarium in Southern Italy.

DEAR ANNE:

Back from Baltimore, where I saw Jack Leaver do several gorgeous operations—and then lose a case he'd set his heart on bringing through. It wasn't his fault—it wasn't anybody's fault, so far as could be discovered. But the patient was a well known bishop of the Church, a man everybody knew and most people loved; nobody had even known he was ill. The news of his death shocked the city. As for Jack —well—I was glad I was there. He felt that all the patient's friends would consider it a case of unnecessary interference, that a man who looked the picture of ruddy health couldn't need an operation, etc.— the sort of thing that gets said when a man marches smiling into a hospital as though he were going to a feast and then in a few hours is carried out again to lie in state in a cathedral.

Poor Jack! Didn't I know? Oh, God—what men of our profession suffer under such circumstances

57

*nobody but themselves and their colleagues under-
stand. It's plain hell. But there's nothing to do except put on a defensive armor of dignified silence and
go on about one's business. I won't try to describe the
indescribable to you. I'll talk of something more
cheerful.*

*And that's a case of interference of a different
sort. You remember Ellen's niece, Sally Beaumont.
Gem of a girl I'd had the pleasure of working over
during her adolescence to make a frail little body
into a sturdy one. I'd done it, too, superbly assisted
by Mother Nature and the great sun god. Anyhow,
I've grown immensely fond of Sally and proud of
her. Getting back from this Baltimore trip, I found
she was on the verge of marrying as rotten a young
scion of a family of good social standing as ever had
the impudence to ask a girl to unite her blood stream
with his in the probability of children that might be
cursed from birth with their unfair inheritance. Of
course, my blood boiled at the thought, and—to
make a long story short—I dashed out to the place
where the crime was about to be committed, held up
the chief criminal at the point of my six-shooter—so
to speak—and stopped everything. No, I can't tell
you all about it, my dear, but your imagination can*

*fill in the details. Luckily, Sally was glad to be
rescued, not on the count on which it was done—
she was ignorant of that—but because she'd let herself be more or less driven into a loveless marriage
by her mother's ambitions—a fine word for it, eh?
She's here now, with me, getting her breath again.
Ellen's still down South, but will be back soon.
Meanwhile, I'm enjoying myself up to the hilt,
though a trifle uncertain as to what I'd better do
next to keep things stirred up!*

*Yes, I know, Anne. You think I'm still a boy and
love nothing so much as cutting a great dash in the
centre of the stage. I'll admit I have a strong sense
of drama and probably ought to have been a cowboy
in the old days of wild adventure on the Western
plains—or a performer in a present-day three-ring
circus. Yet I swear to you that's only one side of me.
The other side is sober enough. An old—and much
older—friend said rather solemnly to me the other
day: "Red, you've never grown up." It set me thinking. Haven't I grown up? Unless one's a moron, can
he help growing up? Especially can one who every
day holds life and death in his hands, and realizes it
with every artery he ties, help growing up? He may
whistle as he goes past the graveyard, to keep his*

courage up—and that of the other fellows who are going past it too—but does that mean that he doesn't make any study of life and its complexities, doesn't appreciate the tremendous forces at work in both the material and the spiritual world, doesn't think—just whistles? My solemn friend has the mistaken notion that whistling is one of the major indications of a hollow head. I hope he enjoys his own long face when he looks at it in the glass.

Enough for this time, Anne, my dear. I hope the slung leg has by now become resigned to its temporary indignity, and that you get sufficient easing of position to make things bearable. It's a mean situation—but think of the enormous relief when it comes down to the level!

Best love,
RED.

II

It was two days before Sally came into Red's private quarters, uninvited and unforced. These quarters consisted mainly of a big square room on the second floor containing a desk and bookshelves filled with scientific treatises of all sorts, with a sprinkling of volumes of history, travel, and adventure. It also had a roomy couch and some easy chairs. There were photographs upon and over the desk.

Red had been tempted to use the bludgeon in getting Sally in, but had resisted. She was accustomed enough to coming to the room, whether Red were there or not, which he mostly wasn't. It was a good place in which to read or write, undisturbed. Sally had been writing letters, these two days, but she had done it in her own room. This evening she had received a telegram. With it she made her way to Red. He had been busy during the days, but he had kept the evenings for her, and he had about made up his mind that if she didn't appear by to-night he was going to be taken alarmingly ill in that room and have her sent for to minister to his needs.

She came in after knocking at the open door. Red looked up from his seat at the desk. He had noiselessly transferred himself to that position, after hearing her door open and close, down the hall. He seemed very much occupied with a letter of his own.

"Shall I bother you?"

He looked up. "Oh, it's you! Not a bit. Just let me make a note or two on what I want to say to this idiot. Take this chair, won't you?"

It was the one near his desk which faced his cunningly arranged trap. But Sally chose to drop into a corner of the big couch, with its inviting pillows, where she read and reread her telegram until Red finished doing that which he was not doing at all.

"All right," said he, putting away his hypothetical work. He took out his pipe and began to fill it. He didn't intend to go and sit on the couch beside her and defeat his own ends. He remained in his desk chair. She could talk across the considerable space if she wished, but he would hang onto his strategic position.

"I've a wire I want to show you," Sally began, looking across at him.

He finished filling the pipe, lighted it, and got it going. He settled back in his chair, with one arm upraised and his hand behind his neck, as though it had an ache in it and needed nursing.

"Fire away," he said.

So she got up and came over. It was the only thing she could do, unless she wished to converse in loud tones, which she didn't. It was stupid of him to prefer to remain in that desk chair, but, of course, if he did she couldn't very well pat the seat beside her and say: "Oh, please come and sit here." Aunt Ellen always let him do as he pleased, after one of his crowded days.

Her thoughts were concentrated on her telegram. She didn't look up at the wall before her—why should she? She was familiar with its appearance; she had studied the varied collection of photographs many times and had heard the story of most of them.

"Uncle Red," she said, "my news may surprise you, but I know you'll think it pretty nice news. I'm sailing for England day after to-morrow with—you never could guess what luck it is—Miss Elizabeth

Stuart. You must remember her? The one teacher I had at school who seemed to me almost the most interesting woman I ever met. She's a real person. She has a cottage in South Devon, on the coast, near Torquay, and she's just running over to spend July and August in it. She understands—well, of course she was sent the cancellation of the—invitation. She wrote me at once, and I wrote back, and then came this wire. It's just too wonderful. If there's anybody in the world I can bear to be with just now, it's Miss Stuart. Except, of course, you and Aunt Ellen. But this will just take me away from everything. I've telephoned Mother, and even she thinks it's a godsend. You think so too—you *know* so, don't you, Uncle Red?"

Crash! All his plans for her in ruins. But he had to play up. He hadn't even heard from Jeff Shipley again. There was no argument to be advanced against Sally's accepting an invitation which she had already accepted. She looked keen about it, too. No doubt, if she was to go away at this time, there couldn't be a finer companion than Elizabeth Stuart. Red knew Miss Stuart. A remarkable person, still comparatively young, spirited, attractive, yet wise and balanced. She would be a tonic for any depression of spirit which must linger for a time, at least, with Sally Beaumont.

"It certainly sounds great," he said, with a forced heartiness.

He hadn't realized how he had set his heart on bringing about his daring schemes. But one couldn't always —or often—stage-manage people about successfully; he knew that well enough. Still—he wouldn't let her get away without a good look at that photograph. Naturally, she wouldn't throw up her engagement with Miss Stuart at sight of it and cry: "Here's the man!" She wasn't thinking about men now, anyway. She was thinking about the South Devon coast, and a small cottage, where people wouldn't surreptitiously look at her and say to one another: "How do you think she's taking it? We all know it was Phil Filmore who did the backing out, only he let her have the honors. When do you suppose he'll marry Dorry Morton?"

"It *is* great," agreed Sally. "I'm so glad you approve. But I should do it, anyway. Nothing so heaven-sent as that could be ignored. My only reluctance is because I shall have to wear—and take . . . No, I vow I won't do that, either. I'll go off in my old clothes."

"Do that, by all means," advised Red. "Give the other stuff away. Or perhaps you'll feel differently about it when you come back. Anyhow, your thinking about what you'll wear is a good sign. The woman who is absolutely in despair leaves the house with only what she happens to have on at the time, even if it's evening dress in zero weather. No, you're still healthy of mind, my dear, thank God!"

"I believe so," Sally assented.

"And here's another healthy person," observed Red, abruptly wheeling about in his chair and looking up at the wall where, with a favorable light upon it from a lamp cunningly turned in that general direction, hung the important photograph. Not at all important now, he feared, yet, by jiminy, he couldn't resist deliberately calling her attention to it, since it seemed the only way to make her see it. "Two of them, in fact," he went on. "Ever see a couple of rougher-looking young brigands? Photograph was sent me not long ago by the younger of 'em—former patient of mine. Don't suppose you know him, but the sight of him gives me such satisfaction I had to hang him and his friend on my wall."

Sally looked at it from where she sat. "Jolly outdoor scene," she commented, without rising from her chair for a closer view. "Where is it? In the Rockies?"

Red wanted to take her by the scruff of her pretty neck and haul her into position before the picture. In the Rockies? What did it matter where it was?

"Northwestern Canada," he explained briefly, and himself rose and took down the frame and handed it to her.

"The one on the right is Leslie Warden, a young British railway engineer. Mighty nice chap. The other's my former patient and special friend—Jefferson Shipley. Doesn't look much like anybody's patient right now, does he?"

"Neither of them does. What a fine face the Englishman has," Sally observed. She seemed to be concentrating on him. If the name of Shipley meant anything to her she certainly hadn't turned a hair at the mention of it. She must know that Jeff was Rivers Shipley's brother, and Rivers had certainly been the shining youth whom Sally in her young girlhood had worshiped afar off and had said she couldn't forget. Jeff looked like Rivers, decidedly—at least, he did in town clothes. Red supposed the outdoor outfit with the high boots was more or less of a disguise.

He was all at once out of patience with his whole absurdly romantic strategy. What of it all now? Sally would be off for England before Jeff turned up, and Jeff would be off for Northwest Canada again before Sally came back.

"So has Jeff a fine face, and a strong one too, to my thinking," he said gruffly, and held out his hand for the picture. But Sally retained it, studying it.

"What a gorgeous job," she said. "No wonder anybody's healthy who lives all the time in a place like that."

"Pretty remote from civilization. Until that road's built there's no way in or out except by plane. They don't come out much."

She asked him details about the construction, seeming much more interested in that than in the two figures of the engineers, with other men at work in the background. He gave such information as best he could, taking out Jeff's letter and reading her the paragraphs of description. When he had finished she rehung the picture herself.

"How many hundreds of miles is that place, do you suppose," she asked, "from a bridge luncheon or a tea? Though I suppose the Englishman has his tea at four o'clock, no matter how far he is out of the world. Having it sitting on a log wouldn't be so bad. What did you say his name was?"

"Leslie Warden," replied Red aloud. In his mind he added: "Hang the Englishman—or are you only pretending he's the one who interests you? These girls—they're *born* equipped with guile."

"Well, I'll soon be having my tea in South Devon," remarked Sally. "You simply can't imagine, Uncle Red, how the thought cheers me! And with Elizabeth Stuart. We'll tramp miles, through those enchanting lanes with the high hedges that I've always been wanting to see again, after once beholding them in apple-blossom time. I must run away now, and write another letter."

She left him. The game was up.

"What an old fool you are, R. P.," he said to himself. "Can't you be satisfied with breaking up a wedding, without trying to make a little Cupid out of yourself, with wings?—*Wings!*"

2

ON THE day of Sally's sailing Red couldn't get away to see her off. Ellen hadn't yet returned. As Sally came down to breakfast he had met her at the foot of the stairs to give her a hug and kiss and tell her that somebody had to be operated upon without an hour's delay. It would probably be impossible for him to reach a train which departed at ten-thirty for New York.

"All my professional life," he said grimly, "I've been finding it necessary to be in one place when I wanted horribly to be in another. So does every other doctor."

"Yes," agreed Sally. "And when you get to heaven all the angels will acquire obscure and frightening pains, and you won't be able to get about to see the place until the day after to-morrow."

"When I get to heaven—" he replied—"if I do— my first request will be to have my telephone disconnected for the first thousand years."

"You'd have it put in again at the end of the first week. But don't worry about me, Uncle Red. I expect nothing less than that you will somehow manage to come tearing down to the train just in time to wave to me on the back platform. I'll be looking for you."

"If I don't I'll write you by the first mail."

"I'll send you back a line from the ship."

"Good enough."

3

BUT he did get there. Of course he did. Red had been making these close connections all his life. He did an unhurried operation, satisfied himself that his patient could be safely left in the hands of the hospital staff—and then cut every corner to get back to his office in time to go with Sally to the train. But Sally had already left.

He was rushing from the house back to his car when a tall, slim figure met him. Hat off, deeply tanned face breaking into a delighted smile, Jefferson Shipley stood before him. For an instant Red didn't know him, in his tailored clothes, and was about to push by with a curt statement that he hadn't a moment to lose and that the young man must look him up some other time, when an amused voice arrested him.

"You don't know me, Dr. Burns—and you're in a hurry, anyway. I'd know you by that, anywhere. So I'll just say I'm Jeff Shipley, and I'll come again."

"What! Why, yes—of course!"

Red did stop stock-still, grasping the hard young hand. Then he smiled quite as broadly as Jeff.

"Come along," he said. "Jump in my car."

"Oh, I won't bother you now."

"Yes, you will. Get in. Don't waste time, man."

They got in, one on either side. The car shot down the street. Jeff took off his flapping hat and held it in his hand. No use trying to keep it on when Dr. Burns was racing for anywhere.

"I'm going to see my niece off for New York. Sailing to-night for Liverpool. Maybe you knew her once. Sally Beaumont."

"Oh," said Jeff, evidently searching his memory. "I think I did, though not very well. One of the youngsters who went to school with my sisters. . . . It seems awfully good to see you, Dr. Burns."

"When did you get back?"

"Two days ago. Been doing the long-lost son with the family. Rivers was home over the week end, and we've done nothing but chin."

"That train's either gone or late," said Red, as they turned a bend in the road which led to the station, on the edge of town. "If she's gone I'll be out of luck. Tremendously fond of Sally, and had to dash off this morning with only time to kiss the tip of her ear as I went by her. There'll be nobody to see her off from here, though there'll be crowd enough at the pier. So I'd rather like to . . . No, it hasn't gone—there's the row of taxicabs at the station. It isn't in sight—always can see the smoke at the tunnel a mile up. Nothing like gambling on train schedules."

He increased his speed. A motorcycle cop, coming up from behind, passed him with a friendly wave back. Red grinned.

"It's always supposed to be a matter of life and death with me," he explained. "The times that chap has looked the other way would have lost him his badge if the town authorities weren't precisely as lenient. This car might be an ambulance or a fire engine; that's why I have an odd-sounding horn. If they mistake me they get the horn."

"It's simply splendid to get back to you, Dr. Burns," Jeff Shipley chuckled. "Everything seems to be speeded up inside of me the minute I see you."

"I ought to get over it—slow down. Can't seem to. It's probably my hair. . . . Here we are, and I hope my Sally's standing patiently on the other side of that station building. Come on."

"She won't care about seeing me——" began Jeff. But a stout arm through his walked him along

beside Red. All right—anything Dr. Burns insisted
on. . . . Just to be with Dr. Burns Jeff would have
gone anywhere.

All the way from the house, no matter what else
he said, Red had been turning over in his mind the
question whether or not he should let Jeff know that
this was the girl picked out for him, by request. For
once in the life of this man of instant decisions, he
was at a loss. There was no time to spin a coin into
the air and then take precisely the opposite course
from the one indicated by the fall of it—as is con-
sistently done by most solitary spinners of coins.
Should he—shouldn't he? Meanwhile, here they
were approaching Sally herself. . . . The first sight
of her gave Red his cue—Jeff wouldn't need to be
told beforehand to take note of her. He wouldn't be
able to forget her. After she had gone, then would
be the time.

She came to meet Red, her face radiant. She
looked, said Red to himself, as adorable as she had
ever looked in her life. He didn't know whether this
was due to her traveling clothes, which gave her the
sleek, poised appearance of the young woman who is
so suitably dressed that she can entirely forget to
wonder how she looks, or because she was really

feeling free and happy in the thought of getting away and of joining a beloved friend for a new adventure. Anyhow, though by now it was only ten days since the episode which had changed everything in her future, she seemed barely a first cousin to the girl Red had watched in the church from behind his pillar. A whimsical thought flashed into his mind: all that cream she had been fed while staying at his home hadn't been wasted; the little hollow in her cheeks had been filled out, her eyes were clear. She was his Sally once more, the most appealing girl he knew.

He made his introduction in a hurry. That train couldn't be far away. Jeff and Sally looked at each other with apparent interest—as why shouldn't they?—and spoke of the days when they had slightly known each other. Jeff mentioned Rivers, his older brother.

"Oh, yes," said Sally, "I remember him, but I was so much younger than he that he'd never remember me. Terribly good-looking and sought after, wasn't he? At my age he seemed to me like quite a god among young men."

"Yes, Rivers seemed that way to me, too. I've never got over it. It was rather a shock when I came

home the other day, after two years in the wilds, to
find my brother not talking the language of the gods
at all, nor looking at me as though I were a barking
pup, but being just an everyday good brother with
all sorts of cares and worries. I'd never supposed he
could have any. He actually seemed to want my
opinion on one or two of his problems. Not that my
opinion was worth anything, but I was very much
flattered. And it made me feel that I'd really grown
up."

"You look very much grown up," Sally assured
him.

Red strolled away. Yet he immediately strolled
back again. He mustn't seem to be throwing them
together. Jeff wouldn't take the opportunity to say:
"Now that I have met you I know what I've been
looking for," or anything like that, and propose getting married before the ship should sail. They
weren't going to meet again. As Red glanced at the
pair he saw nothing to indicate that they wanted to
fall into each other's arms at first sight. He came
up and began to talk, himself, so that Sally would
turn toward him and Jeff could note that really beautiful profile of hers. Yet what was the use of all his
scheming, with the train . . . Yes, it was coming

now, would be here in a minute more. . . . And here it was.

"Good-bye, Uncle Red. Give my very dearest love to Aunt Ellen, and write to me soon. The address is 28, Riverton Road, Torquay, South Devon—probably you'd better send it in care of Miss Elizabeth Stuart. Please put it down so you won't forget."

Red scrawled it on a leaf of his prescription book.

"Good-bye, Mr. Shipley. I hope you'll enjoy your vacation in the States after all that Canadian experience. Yes, porter—those two bags."

"Good-bye, Miss Beaumont. Hope you have a fine summer in South Devon."

The stop, being a suburban, hadn't lasted more than sixty seconds. The train was already moving. Sally stood in the vestibule, looking down, waving at them. Then she was gone, and Red and Jeff turned away.

They walked back in silence to the waiting car.

"Come home with me? We can have a good visit now, if I don't find any calls waiting."

"Thanks. Just back to the house with you, if I may. I left my car parked round the corner. Can't stay, this time. Just drove over in a hurry from our place—got to be back to take a girl I know into town for luncheon and a matinée. But I wanted just to get a look at you, Dr. Burns. It's simply swell to be seeing old friends. Some day I hope we can have a good talk."

"I hope we can," agreed Red, with an odd glance. "I thought you—well—I thought you didn't want to lose any time about that talk?"

Jeff laughed. "A fine, sentimental letter I wrote you, didn't I? Wrote that one evening when the moonlight had got me. Daylight's another thing, eh? You must have thought you had to dry-nurse a baby, when you read that letter."

"You don't look much like a baby."

"I'm sure I sounded like one. Funny how one's notions change, isn't it? My one idea now is to have a jolly time while I'm here and then go back, still a care-free bachelor. Dorry Morton says she'll give me all the fun I want, so we've taken each other on for the summer. She's just about the liveliest thing I could ask for. Used to know her, but had forgotten what a good sport she could be. Mighty pretty, too. . . . So—you don't have to have me on your mind, and I'm sorry I bothered you with my wails about loneliness. Forget 'em if you can. Just the same, I do want to tell you all about the big construction up there in the Northwest and show you a whole raft of pictures and prints, if you care to see 'em."

Red expressed his interest. At the moment he really had no interest in much of anything, least of all in young romance. He was feeling as though someone had knocked him in the head. . . . Dorry Morton . . . the little imp of Satan. He'd like to rescue Jeff from her, yet he couldn't be bothered with any more fuss over other people's affairs. What use? They did as they pleased, and he'd done enough rescuing to last quite a time. He hustled the car over the road, and presently was saying good-bye to Jeff as he sat at the wheel of a very smart open roadster which he said was lent him by his brother Rivers for the period of his stay. He looked the picture of that care-free bachelor, behind that wheel, with his hat-brim flapping in the breeze, and the cigarette he was about to light between his fingers. . . . Dorry Morton . . . what wouldn't she do with this new playmate, eager for a jolly time and thinking he didn't want to marry for a long while yet! Jeff Shipley was just ten times more virile and attractive than Phil Filmore. Dorry would make the most of him, and it wasn't at all inconceivable that she . . .

"Good-bye, Dr. Burns. Thanks a lot for letting me drive to the station with you. May I ring you up some evening and ask for an hour with you?"

"Of course. When my wife is back we'll have you over for dinner some night, if it won't be too dull for you."

"I should say it wouldn't be. Nothing's dull for me. Couldn't be! Why, Dr. Burns, I get a great kick out of just turning the corner on two wheels to dodge the traffic. Traffic's increased forty per cent since I went away. I know I'm a fool over it all. . . ."

He looked back, laughing as he pulled away from the curb. Red understood. Why shouldn't he understand, who had been turning corners on two wheels, both literally and figuratively, since long before he was Jeff's age? A splendid young fellow, capable of hard work and dependable, but just now quite off his head with the exhilaration of getting back to civilization. . . . Dorry Morton, that ruthless young beauty, and Jeff, slightly delirious. . . .

Red went into the house, feeling decidedly depressed. Sally was gone, Ellen wouldn't be back till day after to-morrow. . . .

He went into his big square room, picked up a medical magazine from his desk, disposed himself on his couch, and plunged into an article he had noted before. The title would seem to indicate that the subject was one well adapted to his case. It was: "Common Errors in Diagnosis in Cases Showing Symptoms of Cardiac Lesions."

4

"Now, dear, I'm ready to hear all about it—if you're ready to tell me. Of course I'm immensely interested."

Ellen had finished her unpacking, had had dinner with her husband, and had come upstairs with him into that big square upper room of his where they spent much time together—at his invitation. She seldom invaded it, otherwise. That was one of her theories about married life which had long ago proven its wisdom; a busy man coming home for rest should have one place there which belonged to him exclusively—not merely theoretically, with everybody coming into it, offering one excuse or another—or none at all—because it was so comfortable, livable, and withdrawn. As a result, Red was always insisting on his wife's joining him there, as now.

He sat beside her on the roomy couch, his pipe lighted. He had already told her some dozen times how glad he was to have her back, and had demonstrated it. After all, though he had enjoyed having Sally Beaumont about, even a girl like that couldn't touch his wife for satisfying companionship, he thought. Ellen was a picture to-night, anyhow, in her simple dinner dress of the gray-blue she loved best to wear, with a smoky necklace of lusterless blue crystals dropping from neck to lap.

He hadn't written her the story, in his letters during her absence. It would have taken too many sheets. So now he told it to her in his own concise and graphic fashion, without much wasting of words. She listened, her dark eyes and mobile face showing now surprise, now amusement, and again a touch of concern.

But she was smiling as Red finished and glanced round at her. He had been looking straight ahead as he talked, with occasional pauses to revive the draught in a pipe which seemed to be acting badly.

"Well?" he questioned. "I suppose the whole thing sounds as crazy to you as it does now to me —I admit it. But, nevertheless, I'm not sorry for one minute that I stopped that wedding."

"Neither am I. You are probably the only person in the world who would have thought it could be done, at the last minute, or would have had the courage to do it—unless there were really—what do the courts call it?—cause for action."

"If there wasn't cause for action I don't know what would have been. The women's hospitals are full of the consequences of not having stopped such marriages."

"I know. And I'm thankful our Sally is safe. We shall never understand how she could have been willing to marry Phil."

"Easy enough. Your own sister——"

"Yes, Evelyn is incurably sentimental, and she was determined that Sally should make what was to Evelyn herself an advantageous marriage. But I'm glad I wasn't here. You were perfectly equal to the situation yourself. You say Sally was looking well when she went away? Nothing could have been better for her than a stay in South Devon with that intelligent and stimulating woman, Elizabeth Stuart. Sally will come back with a perfectly sane outlook upon life, and she'll never make such a mistake as that again."

"No—I hope not. But I haven't told you the

whole story, even yet." There was an odd look on Red's face as he turned it toward her, rather like that of a schoolboy who is coming to the worst of a confession he has bravely started out to make.

"Not yet? Do go on. I have a suspicion, dearest, that you've been getting into mischief."

She didn't look as though it worried her. She was quite used to hearing of the extraordinary things that it suddenly occurred to her resourceful and impulsive husband to do. She wouldn't have him otherwise. Never had her married life been dull, nor would it ever be so for lack of surprises of one sort or another.

"I have. But I don't think I've done any harm. I've merely proved myself once again an incurable producer of the dramatic and unexpected. Never shall get over it."

"I hope you never will."

So he told this second story, of Jeff Shipley and his letter and the photograph, and of the complete failure of his own plans. Over this recital she did her best to be properly sympathetic, but she had a hard time of it, and her soft, uncontrollable laughter as he finished with the portrait of Jeff enthusiastically returning to Dorothea Morton while Sally sailed away out of reach, neither of them having appeared to take any special note of each other, made Red sit up in mock despair.

"Yes, I knew you'd laugh at me. I'm an old blunderer, thinking I can pull the strings and make the puppets dance. All I've done is to play into the hands of that young imp, Dorry Morton. She'll make a fool of Jeff, see if she doesn't."

"I don't believe she's so dangerous, Red. Just a staccato young thing having all the fun she can."

"Isn't she, though! She's the sort that takes husbands away from wives. Not so young, either—old enough to be plenty dangerous. Maybe I don't know dynamite when I see it. And I'll hear it, soon enough, in Jeff's case. A loud explosion."

"I thought you said it was Phil Filmore she——"

"Not when she gets a sight of Jeff. Any girl would throw a Filmore over at the altar to marry a Shipley. If you don't believe it, just recall Phil's doughy features and then look at this."

He took down the framed photograph from the wall and gave it into his wife's hands. She studied it carefully.

"He does look very unusual and interesting. So does the other young man, in a different way. But I don't see how you can do anything more about it. You can't go around warning these boys and girls whom not to marry and then presenting them with more desirable alliances. You see, you're so used to issuing orders——"

Red groaned. "Yes, I see. And I give this case up. As a matter of fact, I don't care a hang now who marries anybody. But I had to tell the awful tale and get it over. Now I can settle down and say a few things to my wife that have been accumulating during the month and that I couldn't get on paper. . . . After all, darling . . ."

But before he said them he got up and closed the door. Those intimate things he wanted to say were not to be overheard by any curious maid lurking in the hall outside. He had caught the soft sound of footsteps, and he understood curious human nature all too well.

5

JEFF did come to dinner, upon invitation; did talk about the big job in Canada; didn't say a word about girls! He seemed the exact opposite of the

young man who had written Red of his hope to find
a possible wife. It was as though, as he himself had
said, he felt he had in that letter unwarrantably
shown a soft and emotional side of his nature to a
man who, while he wouldn't laugh at him, would
nevertheless think considerably less of him for mani-
festing it in that way. Anyhow, he now seemed anything but emotional or soft. It was great fun to be
back, he said, but after all he wouldn't mind in the
least when the time should be up, and the Canadian
Pacific bearing him off to the edge of the wilds again.
It was a great adventure, and it wasn't counting
time out of his life in the very least to be spending
his early twenties in this way. If it were only to be
with Leslie Warden . . . and he again expressed
his admiration for the Englishman, seeming to be
unable to rate him too high or present him too
attractively to his own friends.

"I wanted most awfully to bring him home with
me, since he's rather unattached, from what he says,
to any special place. His family are scattered, he
merely goes back to England as Englishmen seem to
—out of sheer fondness for their country. But he
wouldn't come, and countered by asking me there
with him, to go on a walking trip—which is his idea

of a good time, like the postman who spent his holiday on a nice long hike. Now I—the more and faster miles I can cover in my brother's motor while I'm here the better. I may temporarily lose some hardness from the muscles in my calves, but I'm making that up in getting everywhere I want to go and seeing everything I want to see. Blame me, Dr. Burns?"

"Hardly, Jeff. Go to it, with my blessing. Well do I know what fast miles mean to youth—and even more to middle age, if you'll believe it."

Jeff looked at him, laughing. "Middle age! If ever I saw youth it's in your face. You'll never grow old."

"Won't I, though! And why should I want to be a case of arrested development? I don't. Every year I grow richer in experience. I'm willing to pay for it with all the signs of age."

"Speeding isn't one of the signs of age," laughed Jeff.

"Oh, yes, it is. A sort of last whirl, in the air, before the sere and yellow leaf falls to the ground."

Both Ellen and Jeff were much amused by this, as anyone who looked at Red was bound to be. The dinner proceeded with much lively talk, but not a word did Red hear to satisfy his curiosity as to his protégé's doings. When Jeff shook hands, saying good-night, he appeared to realize that he was being unexpectedly reticent and made up for it with one grave little speech.

"Dr. Burns, I thought I'd want to tell everybody everything, when I came home. Perhaps it's the influence of Leslie, who tells nobody anything, but I seem to have crawled into a sort of shell while I've been here. That doesn't seem to fit with what I've said about wanting to see and do everything while I have the chance. But, on my word, I'm seeing and doing it from a window in that shell—which must be on wheels. . . . Somehow, I can't explain. . . ."

"I think I can, Jeff. Your real heart is in your job in the Northwest. You're here almost as an outsider, and you didn't expect to feel that way. I congratulate you on work that absorbs you like that. Other things can come later. Go back, and thank the Lord for your enthusiasm over important interests. They're the sort you need most now."

Jeff gave his hand a terrific pressure—which testified to the fact that no muscles of his had lost their power in these few weeks of vacation—and went away. He said he would come again. So he did, but not until just before he went back to Canada. The short visit, when it took place, was one to be remembered.

6

MEANWHILE, there were occasional letters from Sally Beaumont, in South Devon. She was having—at first—a quiet, peaceful, but delightful time, roaming about the incomparable country with Miss Stuart, or motoring with her in a tiny English car. Then the letters changed in tone: things weren't, apparently, quite so peaceful, but had become decidedly more amusing. She hadn't time to say much, there were so many plans on foot. They were seeing a good deal of a number of Miss Stuart's charming English friends, who were asking them for weekends here and there at pleasant country places. Miss Stuart had so many friends. . . .

Then came the letter which sent Red straight up into the air: at first in a rage of disappointment. Then, as he calmed down under Ellen's gayly teasing comments, he began to accept the situation, and finally to agree that it's probably better not to try too hard to arrange other people's affairs for them, for the simple reason that it generally can't be done. In the end . . . but it was Jeff who had to do with that ending.

Meanwhile, Red was reading and rereading the letter. It began abruptly with an announcement:

"You won't believe it, and maybe you'll be quite shocked, but that won't do you any harm, Uncle Red—you've been shocking people all your life. I'm to be married to-morrow, here at Miss Elizabeth's cottage, to Leslie Warden. You must know a lot about him through your friend Jeff Shipley. It was Jeff who introduced us. He wrote to me, and he wrote to Leslie, who has been staying—he has no home now—not far away at a little country inn. You remember I saw his photograph at your house, and something about his face, as I noticed it even then, made me remember him. When he came to call he brought Jeff's letter. Since then I've seen other letters of Jeff's, telling Leslie that when he saw me at the station and learned that I was going to South Devon, it seemed to him that if we two could meet . . . Well, so it turned out. Can you imagine such a conspiracy? . . . Leslie is thirty-two and has led rather a lonely life; Jeff was convinced that he should marry. Leslie's very fond of Jeff—says he's such a nice boy. He really must be, though I didn't notice him much at the station. I was so anxious to spend the last few minutes just with you that I rather resented his being there. Of course, I'm glad enough now that he was.

"I hope you don't think this is all too hasty. Miss Stuart doesn't, even though I'm going straight back with Leslie, landing at Quebec and taking the Canadian Pacific across to the place where we go in by airplane. I'm not a bit afraid of the rough life— Leslie's made it sound as rough as he could, to scare me. It will be a relief to be on such a new adventure, and—I don't mind putting this in, for your and Aunt Ellen's peace of mind—I love him so very much that anywhere with him would be the perfect place for me. He's the real, real thing, you see.

"I've written Mother to ask her to run up to Quebec and meet us—I hope she will. You all will understand that I couldn't come home for a wedding —not after . . . Uncle Red, I can never be grateful enough to you for saving me from the most awful mistake I could have made—saving me for this. I've told Leslie the whole story, and he says I can't be half as grateful to you as he is."

Red laid down the letter. "The next time I gamble," he said, "it won't be on the favorite, but on some long-legged, rangy dark horse."

7

IT WAS only a day later that Jeff Shipley pulled up his car at the Burns's curb and dashed in. He had a letter in his hand as he was ushered into that upstairs room where Red and Ellen sat. Red got up. Ellen, smiling, put out a friendly hand.

"I see you have a letter," Red said.

"Yes. Have you?"

"I believe there's been one, that we've read several times over. It was an interesting letter. Is yours the mate to it?"

"Of course. Isn't it the greatest news you ever had?"

Jeff's face was beaming. Red scanned him closely.

"So you're pleased?"

"Pleased! I'm quite off my head about it. Good Lord, I made the match! I did it with my good American nerve. The minute I saw that girl on the platform and heard she was going to South Devon I thought of Leslie. Somehow she looked to me exactly the girl for him."

"But not for yourself?" Red couldn't resist this.

Jeff laughed. "Oh . . . she was a lovely thing —I could see that. But I'm not thinking of marrying—yet. . . . You may not believe that, but I really am not—not yet. I've made up my mind I'm probably too young. Too many girls interest me— just for the time I'm with them. I thought I'd be shy and awkward with girls when I got back, but it seemed to be like swimming—if you'd once learned how . . . well, you could at least keep afloat!"

He did look younger—much younger, for some reason, than when he had first come home. He was a nice boy, no doubt of it—but he was still a boy. Sally had had enough of boys; she should have a man. Evidently she now had one.

"Yes, I imagine you've kept afloat," said Ellen.

"Even been able to take a few feeble strokes and get yourself about," added Red.

"A few. Pretty feeble, though."

Jeff caught sight of the framed photograph and went over to it. He took it down, brought it over to Ellen, and sat upon the couch beside her.

"Dr. Burns has done us a lot of honor," he commented, "sticking us up there. . . . Have you looked hard at Leslie, Mrs. Burns? Can you *get* just what he's like? Of course you can't, but it's there. Your Sally will be as safe with him—and as happy. . . . Wait till I get out there too. I'll report back on the case. I promise you my eyes'll be wide open."

"See here," said Red. "It just suddenly strikes me that your friend Warden was engaged to another girl—was to marry her. How about it? Isn't that being off and on again rather rapidly?"

"It may seem so," Jeff admitted. "When he got home he found she'd just married another man— somebody who wouldn't ask her to go out of the world to live. The letter telling him about it didn't reach him before he sailed. I don't think the blow hit him very hard; she'd held him off a long time. And when he saw Sally—well——"

"Caught on the rebound, as the ancient saying has it," commented Red. Sally too, he said to himself. And sometimes the rebound turned out better than the original throw.

"I'm sure it's all right," Jeff assured him.

"I have an idea it is. When are you going?"

"About a fortnight after they do."

"Don't you think you'll be envious?"

"Envious? More than likely. Yet—to tell the truth . . ."

"You'd better," commanded Red. "After all the pondering and anxious thought I put into your case before you came home."

"Oh, did you? What a letter that must have been! . . . Well, then—Leslie's having his sister out, in the spring. I've seen her picture. Les made me promise by all that's crazy that I'd wait till I'd seen her before I . . . In fact, she and I've had some correspondence—awfully interesting. So . . ."

"I'll advise you on one thing," said Red. "Don't decide anything—*anything*—that has to do with your future, on a moonlight night in spring."

"No," promised Jeff, "I won't. That is—if I can help it. You can't sit indoors with them on moonlight nights. They always want to be taken out."

"Take her out," suggested Red, "when it's raining and you both have to wear rubber boots."

"Do you really think that would make any difference?" inquired Jeff, with an engaging cock of the eyebrow.

"No—and God bless you," said Red.

His eyebrow was cocked too.

LETTER from Dr. Burns to his sister, Anne Sutherland, in a sanitarium in Southern Italy.

DEAR ANNE:

It's good news about your mending injuries, but I can't say I'm pleased with your putting on ten pounds of weight. That comes from having to lie in bed and not being forced to restrain your appetite. Don't I know what your trays are like, you having the means to pay for any extras that take your fancy? Cut down the sweets, Anne—cut 'em down till it hurts! You're too young still to be willing to waddle when you get about again, and anyhow, for one of your physical type, that way lie Bright's disease and other insidious ills, too frequently heralded by just that plump pink-and-whiteness which is so attractive till it gets out of hand. Hear me? All right, my dear. But heed me, also—I vow you must, with this prolonged physical inactivity to help the bad work along.

Well, I suspect I made several kinds of an ass of myself, trying to steer Sally's life for her. But out of it came what looks like a promising marriage for her, though not to the man I picked for the part. When it came down to it she did her own picking, which was as it should be, and the Red Peppers of this world should learn a lesson by it. Parents, too.

Why should I be so anxious to get a girl married after getting her out of it? Am I an incorrigible romanticist, in spite of all I know to make me cynical? It must be because there's no use in ignoring the laws of human existence and its perpetuation.

But, you know, Anne, it's rather a terrible thing to try to handle other lives, in any way. A red-head like me is always tempted to use the power he has over people to make them do what he thinks is the thing for them. Suppose he succeeds. Suppose I'd managed to get Sally tied up to the wrong man. I know I was right in pulling her loose from the other —he simply wasn't fit. But attempting to bring about a combination that looked fine and promising to me was what I shouldn't have done—and I'll probably try to do it the next time I get a chance!

Now, here are you, writing me about Dick's supposed "desertion" of you, leaving you to recuperate in that sanitarium while he goes off on that expedition with a bunch of men instead of on the trip you'd planned to take together. You want to know what I think of it. So here's another opportunity for me to mix myself up in other people's affairs by telling you what I do think of it—as of course I shall.

I think it's all right, old girl. He couldn't do much for you if he were there, and you've trotted around so much together all these years, it may be a good thing to let him loose for the three months your doctors say are going to be necessary. You see, your and Dick's case has been very different from Ellen's and mine. No children, plenty of money, both of you fond of dashing about, etc.—you've really done more things together in ten years than the average married pair do in a lifetime. But they've all been conventional things, Anne, do you realize it? You've lived a hotel-steamship-motor-hotel-steamship-motor life. Even when you're at home (do you know the meaning of the word?) you're in an apartment hotel, with everything done for you. Your travel has all been of the luxurious type. You've never roughed it for a day—no, I swear you haven't, my dear girl. I know you think you have, but it's been with servants and camels and caravans to transport you. Now, for once, old Dick has gone off to try how it seems to be where white flannels, dinner coats, and top hats (I don't mean worn all at the same time!) won't be needed. I'll bet he had a great time buying his outfit—got a lot of stuff he'll discard, of course. He'll be another Dick when he joins up with you again— and I have an idea you'll be another Anne. This is the first time you've ever had to lie by in your gay life, isn't it? Maybe you and Dick will try something new together, some day. Settling down for part of the year in a house of your own—perhaps adopting a child. Yes, I know I'm on dangerous ground, Sis. But while you have all this spare time to think things over, think that possibility over. You know, it would be mighty hard for Ellen and me to say which we love the most, adopted Bob, the dear rascal, or Betsy and Nancy, who are really ours. We might never have had a son of our own. A calamity that would have been, too.

Well, I've got to run over and see Max Buller. Remember Max, the best ever? Of course you don't —he's not your sort. He's my best friend, in the profession or out of it, after Jack Leaver, and he's been overworking for so long he's almost committing suicide. I'm worried about him. I'm not worried about you—if you promise to cut out those sweets.

I'll wager there's a box of chocolates on the table by your bed this minute, eh, Anne? If there is, give them to the nurses—they need energy if they're looking after you!

I'm dodging the book you're throwing—you can't hit me. Good-night, Anne, dear.

RED.

III

I WISH, Dr. Burns," said Mr. George Graham, taking final leave of his surgeon as he left the hospital for his big black motor waiting outside, "you would let me do something for you besides this— ah—fee. I'm sorry you wouldn't let me make it larger. You have earned———"

"Oh, never mind," said R. P. Burns, M. D.— thus his office sign read—"you've given me a lot of fun. Your case—man, there've been barely a dozen of them in the history of surgery. I'm no end grateful to you for getting that peculiar and enormously interesting pain of yours almost outside my office door. Think of it—rushing through this town as you were in your car—never here before—probably never here again—you had the generosity to a perfect stranger to double up into a hard knot as you did right here and nowhere else. Why, I ought to do something for you———"

"You can," interposed Mr. Graham, grasping his opportunity, as he was accustomed to do. That was what made him a competent executive in his own world of business affairs. He didn't look the part. He was a thin little man of fifty or so, perfectly dressed, but with no special air of authority about him—unless you caught him in his chair at the head of a board of directors' table, where, when he spoke in that quiet, almost hesitating way of his, the others invariably listened, and with reason. They were usually sorry when they hadn't.

"How can I?" Burns inquired suspiciously. He scented philanthropy, and he would have none of it as concerned himself.

"I have a camp in the hills," said Mr. Graham, "not fifty miles from here. I'm not going to use it this season. The weather is growing hot—it will be hotter. You need a rest—all doctors do, according to my observation. If you would do me the honor——"

"One of those gilt-edged camps, I suppose," suggested Burns, with a friendly but distrustful smile. "Silk quilts on the beds, and bathrooms all over the place."

"The silk quilts can be put away and red blankets substituted, if you prefer. It's just a comfortable, good-sized cabin, and not at all gilt-edged, as you

think, Dr. Burns. It can be made ready in a day, if
you'll allow me to wire——"

Burns was about to shake his head, explaining
that he needed no vacation. Then, suddenly, he
thought of his friend, Dr. Maxwell Buller. *There*
was a man who did. If this Graham really meant
it . . .

He inquired into it carefully. When he and his
late patient parted, the thing was all arranged. The
slender executive and the hair-trigger surgeon had
seen eye to eye concerning the welfare of Burns's
best friend in the profession, the hardest working,
most vacationless, nearest worn-out physician the
village had.

"I shall take great pleasure," said Mr. Graham,
in his quiet, soft-voiced way, "in thinking of Dr.
Buller's occupying the camp. And if you, Dr. Burns,
will spend some time there with him . . ."

"I'll have to," Burns admitted. "The old dog
wouldn't stay there a week if I didn't. He'd limp
back after me—maybe die on the way."

Mr. Graham went away contented. He had heard
tales from his nurses as to Dr. Burns's working
himself to death. Vigorous as he still seemed in the
middle forties, they were afraid they'd some day

lose him. Mr. Graham had gathered that no calamity could hit the hospital at which the red-headed surgeon was chief operator, like that.

2

BURNS had a tussle with Maxwell Buller. Buller had been the man who had had to deal a smashing blow to Red, at the time of the Great War, by telling him a tale about his heart. Which organ, though good enough, more than likely, for years more of work —he was then thirty-three—wouldn't get by the inquiring stethoscopes of the examiners at the recruiting stations. The tables had been turned: it was now Red who had to tell Buller a few things neither of them liked to mention.

"But I can't get away, Red."

"You've got to get away, Max."

"I can't."

"You must."

"No. Mrs. Pike—old John Nevers—the Brewster twins——"

"You're going." Red Pepper picked up Buller's telephone.

And at that particular moment, as though Nature

took a hand in the argument, Buller suddenly went gray in the face, and his friend Burns had to do some quick work upon him. Which settled it. Buller had hoped Red would never catch him in one of those moments of collapse from overfatigue, but now he had, and it was the end of the discussion.

3

"NICE place," said Red, lighting his pipe. "Not my idea of a camp, exactly, but then these bankers have no idea of doing anything halfway or even a quarter way. None too soft for you, though, Max."

Buller looked about him, from where he lay in a sort of glorified deck chair, all cushions and comfort. The two were upon the long porch which looked off into the dark summer night. Not a light to be seen anywhere. Cool and comfortable it was here; ninety-five all over the lower country to-day, according to the evening paper, which Brown, the camp caretaker, had lately brought up. It couldn't be more than a mild eighty here. And a little breeze blowing which made it seem cooler.

"I've given in to you, Red," said Buller, "because I don't seem to be able to fight you."

"People usually can't," Red chuckled. Concerned though he was over Buller, he had immensely enjoyed putting through the business of getting him up here. It had taken less than a week to bring it all about.

"But I still don't feel right because your wife and children aren't here."

"Will you quit that? Ellen herself told you they a lot preferred the seaside—were all set to go, anyway. What those youngsters would do if they couldn't tumble around in the water, I don't know. They're all settled in. Bob's crazy over getting himself browner than he already is—if possible. The two small 'uns took along enough shovels to dig up the entire coast line. As for Len—it's a good thing for her to get away from her Red-head for a while—and me from her, if you want to know it."

Buller looked around at his friend in amazement.

Red laughed. "Say it," he commanded.

Buller couldn't say it. He wasn't married himself —never had been. To him Red and Ellen Burns were the most successfully married couple he had ever known, and he hadn't known many he could call that. Mrs. Burns—well—he had never discovered anybody like her. Still young and lovely at—she

must be in the late thirties—and charming past
description. He understood beyond a doubt that Red
was devoted to her—no man in his senses wouldn't
be. Buller had envied Red all these years—and Red
was the only man he had envied.

"What an old conservative you are," mused Red.
"A dyed-in-the-wool bachelor, and then shocked
beyond expression because I say a thing like that.
Why, man, the life and breath of marriage are the
temporary separations in it. Every so often, ever
since we've been married, Len packs her trunk and
goes off down South, where she came from. I hate
like the devil to see her go, because the Lord knows
I never get enough of her in the intervals between
patients. But that makes no difference with her.
Away she goes, stays a month, perhaps, and comes
back. When she gets off the train and I see those
black eyes of hers again—well—I go mad with joy,
precisely as I did that day so long ago, when I married her. And—let me tell you—since I know what
you're saying to yourself this minute—it's only
partly because she brings with her the faintest,
subtlest sort of a breath of fragrance, one I
associate with the very beginnings of things. It's
much more because I feel—complete again. I'm all

there when she comes home—and only half there when she's away."

A deep sigh from the stretched-out shadow in the darkness which was Maxwell Buller was the answer to these descriptions of something he knew, by personal experience, nothing about. Red heard it and responded instantly and characteristically:

"The devil take me for saying that sort of thing to you, old boy."

"I don't mind what you say to me, Red. Go on. I like to hear anything you'll tell me. I—you know it isn't often, all these years, we've had any chance to sit down and talk about anything except patients —cases . . ."

It was quite true. The two men had been the best friends in the world, standing by each other through all sorts of emergencies, crises, such as constantly occur in their profession. Red had fought Buller's battles; Buller had in his quiet fashion defended Red when other men, jealous of his popularity and his spectacular successes in the operating field, had been unfair to him.

"I know we haven't. We've got to make up now. Lord, what I owe you! I'll never forget what I thought about you, Max, when I first came to town and into your office. Most of the other fellows I'd called on——funny etiquette, isn't it, to have to go around and present yourself to all the other doctors and tell 'em you're hanging out your shingle——most of them were cool and condescending. But you——I picked you out for a father right then, though you couldn't have been more than a year or so older."

"The reason why they were cool was because you looked dangerous, Red. You did, even to me, though I liked you. I knew you were going to be——" Buller hesitated.

"Cock o' the walk? Yes, I suppose, even then, when I didn't know much of anything but thought my hospital experience had made me fit to take charge of everything, I must have looked and acted like a young madman." Red laughed, thrusting his fingers through his thick hair. "And I *was* one. The surgical stunts I dared attempt——the very thought of some of them makes me cold now."

"Now——when you're still doing twice as complicated——"

"I have my technique now——that's different. And conditions are different. But then——I was a daredevil. I don't know how I got away with as much of it as I did. Many's the time I've come home to

Ellen, so sick at heart I could only bury my head in . . . And next morning went out with that same red head in the air. . . . But that's enough about me. I've learned a few things."

"That red head will always be in the air."

"I suppose so."

"I wish," said Buller presently, "you'd tell me—if you feel like it—a little more about your married life, Red. I've been on the outside looking in so long."

"You ought to have married, yourself, Max. Lord only knows why you haven't."

"Yes," said Buller—he couldn't talk about why he hadn't married—"I suppose the Lord, if He took any interest, was the only one who did know."

"How do we know He didn't take an interest?" Red inquired promptly. "You know, Max, say what they will—some of 'em—I can't get away from that idea. I read their stuff, and now and then it gets me, and I tell myself we don't know anything —never can know anything—fools to think we do, and most of us don't think it, anyhow. And then something happens to make me feel that a bit of solid belief is a lot more real than a mess of shifting doubts—negations. It's something to hang onto."

Buller didn't answer, but his pale face, turned toward Red, bore an expression of gratitude.

Said Red to himself, "That's enough of that. Mustn't preach at him—he'll think I think he's in need of a priest." So he went on in a hurry.

"My married life? It's a wonder any woman could put up with it, eh? I've slowed down a lot now."

"Yes?" Buller had to question that. It was he who had many a time urged the slowing down, only to have his advice set aside.

"Yes, I have, you old tyrant, and you know it. Ellen's seen to that. She's the artfullest woman you ever knew, behind all that sweet calm of hers. She can be the Balm of Gilead and the Spices of Araby, but she can also back me into a corner in this matter of taking care of myself, and I can't kiss my way out of it—not till I've given in."

Buller turned his head away, so the light from inside the window didn't fall on his face. "Can't kiss my way out of it." What a phrase to start a poor fellow's imagination. Many a night he had lain awake, thinking and thinking of the one woman who, since he had known her, had become really the only one of whom he had ever thought with an overpowering longing. That longing, in all these years he had been Red's friend, had never ceased to torment him. And he had never, by word or act or look—when anyone could observe him—betrayed himself. It wasn't in his stern code that he should. There are such men—a very few. Maxwell Buller was one of them. Plain, intelligent face, shoulders a little stooped with care, manner all but shy where women were concerned, but courageous to the depths of his sensitive nature, Buller had his faults, but, after all, was as nearly pure gold as could be found among men. And Red knew it, but he would never know the other thing. As for Ellen . . .

4

BUT they didn't talk any more about Red's married life that night. Red discovered that it was late and bundled Max off to bed. He all but tucked him in, in the luxurious single bed in one of the smaller guest rooms, evidently intended for bachelors. Red was glad of the luxury when it came to beds. He didn't suppose Buller had ever taken the time or trouble to renew springs or mattress on his own; Red had no doubt at all that the crazy old springs and the depression worn in the mattress let the occupant down so that he could all but feel the old-fashioned slats. Buller had been too busy to bother, and he had had no wife to tell him that he might be more comfortable. His office equipment was what it should be, but that was as far as his expenditures went. He hadn't spent many consecutive hours in bed, anyway.

"Pretty soft, eh?" questioned Red, when he had seen his friend under the light blanket which was all the night required up here in the mountains. He actually did want to tuck the blanket in, but fore-bore. He noted with a trained eye how poor a color it was in the face against the white pillow.

"So soft I'm afraid I shan't stay awake long enough to appreciate it."

"Don't. You couldn't do Mr. George Graham a greater favor—nor me, either. Good-night, and don't be asinine enough to pull out for breakfast. I shall probably sleep late myself."

"You'll be up with the dawn," murmured Buller, with another of his involuntary deep sighs.

Red closed the door, shutting a portion of his heart inside. Why did it have to be his best friend who was in such shape as this? Why couldn't it have been Grayson or Fields or some of the others? Good enough fellows, but they couldn't touch Max Buller's little finger for real worth. They played tricks in and with the profession. Buller wouldn't condescend to some of their tactics. So it was he who had to get knocked out—and what did they care? Not a thing. But Red cared so much that he went out and walked the porch for an hour before he went to bed, thinking and thinking, with his teeth clamped down hard on the stem of a pipe which had gone out unnoticed five minutes after he had lighted it. . . .

5

"You're wanted on the telephone, Dr. Burns."

Burns got up. He and Buller had been sitting out on the pine-needle-strewed ground in the sunshine. The heat had moderated considerably, and the smell of the balsams had lured them. They had been in camp nearly a week now, and Red had persuaded himself that Buller looked a shade less like a sick man.

"Familiar sound," the red-head growled, as he had growled a thousand times before. "I wouldn't have a wire left in up here if I dared cut my family off from being able to call me."

He went inside. Buller, lying comfortably in his cushioned deck chair, smiled to himself. It wasn't the family who called Red, it was Red who called the family, every night. He could always be heard booming away, imagining probably that he couldn't be heard outside the room where he was talking. Wanted to know all about what they were doing. Wanted to know if they needed anything. . . .

He was booming now. Impossible not to hear. How well Max knew Red's way of responding. He could never get the preliminaries to a long distance call through fast enough, no matter which end of it he was on.

"What? . . . This is Graham's camp. . . . Yes. . . . Burns—yes. . . . All right—all right—I'm ready. . . . Bob? Yes, boy—what is it?"

A short interval, punctuated by Red's startled exclamations.

"What? . . . What? . . . No! . . . *Oh, God!* . . . But she's all right? Bob—she's all *right?* . . . Are *you* all right? . . . What time did it happen? . . . No bad reaction—sure? . . . Why in heaven's name didn't you call me before? . . . No, of course, you couldn't. . . . You did exactly right, only

I—— . . . Bob, I'm *coming* . . . coming like lightning . . . starting one minute from now. . . . Good-bye, old fellow. . . . I'm proud of you. . . . Yes. . . . Yes! No, tell her I won't break my neck getting there—but I'll get there. Must see her—and you. . . . Good-bye!"

Buller didn't need to see his friend to know that, so to speak, every red hair on Burns's head was electric. Buller had got out of his chair to go to meet him when he heard directions being given inside to Brown.

"Take good care of Dr. Buller. I'll probably be back by night, but don't let him have a lonesome day. Tell him some fishing stories. See he has his eggs and milk and orange juice—pour 'em into him."

Then, outside, Red running down the steps, hatless, pulling on his gray flannel coat as he came. His tanned face flushed, his eyes, as Max had seen them so often, like hazel lights.

"Can't stop to tell you—they're all right—Ellen and Bob. Only I have got to see them—make sure. Back to-night, I think, or to-morrow, at the latest. . . . You don't mind?"

"Of course not. I'm thankful they're all right, whatever's happened. I——"

But Red was off. Leaping into the roadster which had been standing near the porch—he had been starting for the mail shortly—he had got the motor going with a roar and had disappeared around a bend in the steep hill road before Buller had finished the few words he had tried to say. Precisely as of old. Nobody would have believed the man was forty-five. He didn't look it—didn't act it—*wasn't* forty-five—couldn't be. Buller, only a year or two older, felt ninety by comparison. Yet, as for experience, Redfield Pepper Burns had already packed a lifetime of it into his forty-five dynamic years. Compared with him, Buller seemed to himself hardly to have lived at all.

He had an anxious day, in spite of the assurance that everybody was "all right." That was the sort of thing always said to invalids, but the rushing to get to the place where something had happened rather negatived the reassurance. Still, Red seldom walked when he could run: one couldn't tell by that.

It was early evening when Red came back. Buller had had all the lights put on in the cabin's large central room and was waiting there. He heard the powerful motor come up the steep, winding hill through the woods—a low purr, but plainly audible in the night air. He went to the door and stood there. The car came into view, three people in it. Brown went to meet it. Buller was pretty shaky because of the worried day he had spent; he hoped everything really was all right. He watched the three get out of the car—Red and two others. They walked slowly up the path, and their faces grew visible in the light from the house: Ellen, with Red and their son Bob on either side of her. Both had their arms through hers, though she seemed to be walking steadily enough. Both were looking down at her as though there were nothing else to look at.

For herself, as the three came up the steps, she glanced up and saw Dr. Maxwell Buller standing in the doorway, the light behind him, his face hardly perceivable, but the lines of his figure the lank ones she knew. His attitude was one which suggested weakness, for he leaned against the doorpost as though to steady himself. She spoke to him, in the clear, low tones which always thrilled him—him, who was supposed to know no thrills, only plain work and duty and routine.

"How nice to see you here, Dr. Buller," she said. "And I assure you all this escorting by my husband and son is quite unnecessary—though very pleasant."

She was smiling up at him. He couldn't see that anything had hurt her, changed her. She appeared to be as well and certainly as enchanting as always, and there was a hint of sunburn on her clear skin. Her black eyes, softened by their extraordinary lashes, looked to him like velvet, as they always had. It was wonderful to Buller, after a day of imaginings, to see her just as usual. But his heart was beating hard.

Red and Bob released her, and she came up to Buller and gave him her hand. "So very nice," she said again. "And I hope it's doing you and Red lots of good to be up here—such blood brothers as you are. What a delightful place it is! I came up to look it over with Red, you know, but I hadn't seen it all lighted like this."

She seemed to be doing it all. Buller couldn't yet get his throat clear. Red and Bob also seemed struck with silence. Bob, whom Red had adopted when he was still a bachelor and the boy a small orphan of five, had grown into a tall, handsome youth of seventeen, with black eyes and hair so like Ellen's, and a smile so winning, that he might easily have been her son. Red had always insisted that seeing the two together when he had first brought Bob home was what had put the idea into his head that they belonged together—and under his own roof. Though the Burns's had two other children now, little daughters of whom they were deeply fond, this adopted boy had somehow retained his place as the original link between them, and a son in his own right.

Certainly he was behaving like a son now. He shook hands with Dr. Buller, then put his arm about Ellen's shoulders, and was first to speak, for Red appeared to be strangely dumb as yet.

"Shall we go along in and put Mother in one of those big chairs I see in there? Not that she seems to need it—" he was proceeding with her as he spoke, while Red and Buller stood aside for them— "but Dad and I can't stop coddling her to-day."

"Tell you all about it to-morrow, Max." Red had spoken at last, in a queer, gruff voice, such as Buller knew meant strongly restrained feeling. "Going to put her straight to bed now." He went out of the room in the direction of the cook's quarters.

"Of course, there's no use disputing him when he

takes charge," said Ellen lightly to Buller, who shook his head.

"I can testify to that," he said.

He thought he saw slight signs of strain in her face, in spite of her entirely natural manner. Evidently she had been in some sort of danger, and husband and son were hardly more recovered from the shock of it than she. Bob had sat down upon the arm of her chair, and his young arm still possessed her in her loveliness—loveliness—that had always been the word for her in Max Buller's thoughts.

Red came back with a glass on a small tray, and a little plate of wafers. Buller, glancing at him, saw a Red who looked, for the hour, ten years older than he had looked yesterday. Just as he did, his friend thought, when he was operating on a critical case. Then, always, certain mature lines stood out upon his face which one didn't notice at other times: a grave concentration, a sense of heavy responsibility, a stern self-control, repeated at each new and serious situation, had etched them there.

Ellen's husband smiled as she looked up at him and took the glass. Was he still anxious? She smiled back, and then Red's eyes and Bob's met above her head. How they loved her, thought Buller—and wondered if they could possibly love her more than he himself, though nobody knew about that. Why shouldn't he? Who could help it? And at this moment, between his physical weakness and his consciousness that they must all have come near losing her, he was very nearly done for as to strength to keep on sitting there, aloof, unable to touch her, as they could, or to show more than the interest of a good friend. Friend!—He could have died for her, even as Red and Bob.

But that strain was soon over for him. They took her away to Red's own room.

"Good-night, Dr. Buller," she said. "I hope you'll go to bed soon yourself. It's such a deliciously sleepy air up here in the quiet, isn't it?"

"It surely is. Good-night, Mrs. Burns. Please sleep well, won't you?"

"Indeed I shall."

"I give her exactly ten minutes to be at it," Bob called back as the three went out.

But Buller couldn't sleep. He lay awake all night, until, at dawn, he dropped off for an hour. What had life denied him, that he could know its joys and sorrows, its great experiences, only at a sort of second-hand, like this?

6

IT WAS Bob who told him, in the morning, what had happened. Red had insisted on his wife's staying quietly in bed all day, though he briefly reported her to Buller as in fine condition, and added, with a touch of his old whimsical, assured manner, that he had behaved so badly that she had said it was he who ought to be in bed, if anybody must.

"The kid'll tell you what it's all about," Red said, as he left the room. "I don't seem to want to. Funny thing to have the garrulous talker dumb, isn't it?"

"Not exactly funny, Red. Give my—good wishes to Mrs. Burns, please."

Queer, tongue-tied Buller. Any other man would have sent his love. Buller, who had so much love to send, couldn't even use the word.

When he was outside, stretched in his cushioned deck chair in the shade of a group of balsam pines, Bob came out and dropped down upon the fragrant needle-strewn ground beside him. The boy, who was almost a man, sitting with his long, flanneled legs crossed, looked up with a bright face at the too early ageing doctor. Whatever the shock had been to him, he was evidently over it, with youth's elasticity.

"This must all seem a lot of mystery to you, Dr. Buller," he said. "But Dad wouldn't have a word of it told last night, and I'm sure you slept better for not hearing."

"Perhaps," agreed Buller. He was very weary this morning with the nearly sleepless night, but he was anxious to know what had taken place. He wanted to be able to judge somewhat for himself whether the consequences were likely to have any lasting effect.

"Well, it's soon told, just as it all happened in one half hour, though it seemed like a year at the time." The brightness had dropped out of Bob's face. An expression of fine gravity had taken its place. He was about to live again in the day before. One couldn't tell such a story without feeling it.

"We have an awfully jolly little cottage at the shore," he began. "Gray shingles, and a path of flat stones down to where the beach begins. We're quite far from the other cottages. Nearest ours—quite a distance—some people came soon after we did. We didn't know them. A big fat man and a big fat wife —they didn't look interesting in their bathing clothes. They were in the water a lot the first two days. Then the woman stayed out—got too badly burned, we guessed. We noticed them, because Nancy and Betsy—my sisters, you know—made up names for them at once. The Porpoise and the Lobster they called them, and those names tickled Mother and me, they fitted so well. The man had a grayish purple swimming suit, and the woman a bright red one. We all got to alluding to them by those awful names right off. The man swam like a porpoise, rolling along—his fat kept him up, I suppose. The woman couldn't swim much, in spite of her being even rounder and more tubby than the man. You can see we couldn't be much excited about them. They were—at any distance—you might call them commonplace—terribly. Mother insists nobody's commonplace if you know all about their lives. But these people—they were that—to me, anyhow."

Bob seemed to use the word with some reluctance, young aristocrat that he looked, though he had been born no aristocrat. But the marks were there. He was simply trying to make Buller see what was to him an important background to his story. Buller saw. Yes, this man and woman were undoubtedly commonplace. And another woman, whose life was priceless, had somehow almost lost it on their account? He found himself shivering nervously in anticipation.

"I won't make a long story of it." Bob noted how little color there was in Dr. Buller's face and remembered that he was far from well. Dad was staying up here with him on that account. He mustn't be harrowed with elaborate details. The bare facts were enough—if Bob could keep to bare facts. There was a touch of the dramatic in Bob. He wanted to write plays some day, when he should know enough about life. At seventeen Bob didn't think he knew all about life. It was Dad who had kept him from thinking that—Dad who was still, to Bob, a high authority, because, to his adopted son's observation, he had never allowed himself to get into a rut. A rut—Dad!

He went on, trying to be restrained. "Mother loves to get up and take an early morning dip. So do I—when I haven't been out on a late party. There's a crowd of awfully gay young people at the hotel, up the beach. That morning she was out before I'd opened my eyes. She's a marvelous swimmer—not for strength or long distance, but for grace and beautiful diving and all that. Looks like a girl in her swimming things. I don't like to have her out alone, though—never let her, unless she gives me the slip, as she likes to do—especially when it's high tide.

"I woke up that morning—yesterday—with a queer sort of start, as if I'd been called. My room faces the sea, and I jumped up and looked out. At first I didn't see anything—then I heard the call again, high and desperate sounding. I leaned out of my window and finally saw, pretty well out beyond the surf, and in front of the Porpoise's cottage, two heads. Saw them off and on, and couldn't make out who they were, and of course I didn't stop to see. I ran down and out in my pajamas, and I shed 'em as I ran. No time to bother with togs. Queer, but it came to me, as I sprinted, that Mother's door had been open when I went past it, though I hadn't looked in. Then I caught a glimpse of something red out there. My first thought was that it was the Lobster, then I knew it was Mother's red bathing cap. She wears a black suit, but Dad makes her put on a red cap, so she can be seen. Maybe that didn't make me tear along faster!"

Though Bob's voice was low, excitement was creeping into it. And though Max Buller knew that

Ellen was safe, and sleeping quietly in her room up here in the hills, not two hundred feet away from where he and Bob sat, his pulses were hammering.

"Hang it, I can't seem to make a short story of it, Dr. Buller."

"Of course you can't. I want to hear it just as it happened."

Not for nothing had Max Buller, like every man of his profession, been disciplined for many years in keeping his nerves from showing. Bob couldn't see that the perspiration was breaking out all over his listener's thin body.

"Well, then—I got out there just in time. Mother, game as you make 'em, was keeping that old Porpoise's head above water—somehow. He was groggy with what he'd swallowed. He'd got a cramp or something. You see, when she first came out of the house, she'd seen him in trouble—or what she thought might be trouble, though he wasn't calling out—so she'd swum out to him. He was pretty far out. She said she thought she might just have to encourage him a little—he'd seemed able enough to swim other days, in his porpoise way. It was awfully early—nobody was up, not even the man's wife. No life guards around at that hour—

they are farther up, by the hotel, anyway. When Mother got there she realized she had a real rescue on her hands, and it was then she called—and I'd heard her. Not even the Lobster did. To do him credit, he wasn't hanging onto her enough to pull her under; seemed to have sense enough left to know he mustn't do that. But he couldn't straighten out his legs to swim, and he was half strangled. She was trying to keep his head above water—she couldn't possibly have brought him in alone. Just how long she could have kept him up there's no knowing. He was purple in the face, and she was pretty white when I got there, and you know———"

Bob was suddenly silent a minute, and something worked a little in his throat. Then he got the better of it and went on:

"I haven't the least idea she'd ever have let go. She'd have hung onto him till he lost enough of his own pluck to—grip her too tight. You can't imagine what—my mother is, Dr. Buller."

Couldn't he? Hadn't he seen her when years ago Red had fought through weeks of a frightful infection, and not one of all his physicians had thought he could pull through; keeping her courage, her poise, her gallant smile? Hadn't he seen her when her children had been dangerously ill, showing the poise and endurance and quiet fortitude which had enormously re-inforced the efforts of the doctors and nurses? Didn't he know how that silken sweetness and charm of hers covered a will like that of a soldier? Yes, he knew. He too knew that she would have hung on. That both the Porpoise and the Sea Gull might have been to-day at the bottom of the sea . . . or . . . washed up on the beach. And that his friend Red would have wanted to go out and lie beside her, as still as she. He knew, and clenched his thin hands on the arms of his chair. He too . . .

7

Bob hurried on, evidently trying to be matter-of-fact after this one touch of honest emotion. It *had* been a close shave, no doubt of that, and he couldn't forget it.

"You see I hadn't dared stop to try to get a boat. None near by, though up by the hotel there were two or three big speed boats and a small outboard motor or two. And when I got out to Mother I saw she was in no shape to swim in alone, even if I could have managed to knock out the Porpoise and tow him in by myself. So I made her let me take him off her hands, gave him enough of a wham under the jaw to stop his struggling, and kept him afloat while I let out some of the wildest Indian yells you ever heard. Mother was floating, and said with what breath she had left she was all right, but I couldn't trust her. I watched her every minute and, believe me, I'd have let the Porpoise go in one split second and taken her in if I'd seen she needed it."

"Yes . . ." breathed Max Buller. He could see it all.

"And at last the Lobster heard me. She came tumbling out of the house, and her yells joined mine with a vengeance. She had on some kind of flapping red kimono over her nightgown, and she began running up the beach toward the hotel, shrieking as she went. And just about then, when it had begun to seem hopeless, the whole beach woke up. In five minutes more there were two speed boats and a row-boat—fisherman's from around the bend the other way—all piling toward us. People were shouting, and the boats were tooting, and the war was over. And Mother, lying on her back, close to me, all ready to come back on the job and try to help me in case I needed it, said: 'It looks as though we were going to get back in time for breakfast after all, Bobby.' Can you beat that?"

Buller didn't need to reply. He didn't try.

"Well, that's all of it. They got Mother and me into one boat and hauled the Porpoise into another—they estimated he weighed about two hundred and seventy, counting the brine he'd swallowed. There was a welcoming committee on the beach, and it was just about when I saw it that I realized I wasn't exactly dressed to be welcomed. You remember I'd dropped those pajamas on the beach. The men in the boat fixed me out, though they weren't very thoroughly clad themselves. At least I had somebody's shirt draped round my loins and tied by the sleeves."

"Your mother—when you got her in . . . ?" questioned Buller. It was even yet as though he didn't know she was safely sleeping only those two hundred yards away.

"Oh, two huskies made a chair of their hands and carried her to our cottage. I'd have preferred to do it myself, playing the hero part in my borrowed shirt. But instead I found myself being hoisted up —only I got away. One benevolent old fellow—he must have slept with his hip flask on him to have had it on hand so early in the morning—came in and insisted on giving us both a bracer. It brought back the color to Mother's face in a jiffy. . . . As for the Porpoise, you know I wouldn't have left telling about him to the last if he hadn't been in fair enough shape to be turned over to the Lobster. He'd just about come to when we got to land, and I'll say he'd had rather the best time of the three of us, having nobody on his mind to be worried over except himself. He and the Lobster came over later in the day, and somehow, when they were stumbing over their thanks, they didn't seem quite so commonplace after all. I was glad they hadn't been separated for good, they seemed to think such a lot of each other."

"Then you called your father," prompted Buller.

"I did, after I'd got a doctor over from the hotel to make sure Mother was all right. He said she was, only needed rest, so I could tell Dad that. I knew he'd come, just the same. When he reached there he—well—I guess I'd better not go into that. You can see for yourself how the whole thing got him."

Buller nodded. Being on the outside looking in

is an amazing stimulus to the imagination. He closed his eyes.

"So here we are, and it's a great morning to be alive in," ended Bob cheerfully, getting up and dusting pine needles from the gray-flanneled legs. "I'm going to wander down that trail and let you rest. It's going to do you a lot of good to be up here, Dr. Buller."

Buller opened his eyes. "Yes," he agreed. "Only don't let anything like this happen again, Bob."

"You bet I won't, if I have the whole coast guard out when my pretty mother gets up early to go in swimming."

"You're—both—going back?"

Bob looked his amazement. "Why, of course, when Dad's satisfied Mother's done nothing to hurt herself—as of course she hasn't. She could have managed anything that wasn't a ton of blubber— she's saved at least three kids from drowning, and one or two women, in her time. I'll admit they were nearer shore than the Porpoise, but she's mighty fit, you know—Dad's kept her so."

Bob strolled away. Buller presently went to sleep from sheer exhaustion. Even listening may be arduous when one is very nearly down and out.

8

NEXT morning Red was himself again. He came in and sat on the edge of Buller's bed—breakfast had been sent in for the guest, and he had just finished it. Red had insisted that Buller should permit this much of what the invalid called coddling. Buller hadn't been running any temperature except when overtired, or Red wouldn't have let him out of bed at all.

"Len's fit as a fiddle," he announced. "She wants to come in to see you. They're going back this morning. Brown will drive them down."

"So soon?"

"Len's got the babes on her mind. Left 'em with Celia and a friend of hers, who could be trusted with heirs to the British throne, if necessary. But it seems there's a children's party on at the hotel to-morrow, and Len wants to see 'em enjoy it. Besides, she insists on leaving you and me together. Got to let her have her way."

"You don't dread having her back there again, where——"

"Why, what's scaring you, Grandmother? Of

course I dread it. That's why I'm letting her go.
Len wouldn't stand for being kept from it, and I
know better than to try. Don't these flying fellows
who come down after making a near thing of it go
straight up again to get back their nerve?"

"Yes—I understand. But I hate to have you kept
up here with me when she——"

"Now, just get over that. That's what she wants
to see you about."

"I'll get up and dress."

"No, you won't." Red's fingers explored his
friend's wrist. "I'm not sure but this little episode
has been harder on you than on any of us. Inaction
always is, in crises. Anyhow, in bed you stay till
noon, anyhow, and Len will be in in fifteen minutes.
That'll give you time to have Brown shave you and
put some perfume behind your ears."

It sounded like the old Red again, and Buller had
to submit.

9

ELLEN BURNS came in alone presently. She did
look "fit as a fiddle," and there was no cause for the
invalid guest to feel any more concern about her. He
was almost glad she was going back. He couldn't

have stood much more of having her under the same roof with him. It was undermining to that obstinate will of his, which had even set itself not to allow him to think about her and Red together. Worn out though he was, he still was a man; this woman was the one the very thought of whom had for years made it hardest for him. She was so lovely . . . so lovely. . . .

She sat down by his bed. He knew his hand had been icy cold and maybe a little damp when he had taken her warm one in it. But he couldn't help that, though he hated the realization. She looked fresh and young, her black eyes rested on his thin face with a beautiful friendliness in them, as always. She wore some sort of apple green sports clothes, with a little green hat; he thought they suited her, as whatever she wore did suit her.

"Max," she began—and paused. His unsteady pulses had started at the sound of his Christian name on her lips. She saw his surprise, and smiled. "It's absurd that we should have gone on calling each other Dr. Buller and Mrs. Burns, in the old-fashioned way, all these years, when you and Red are such tremendous friends. Now that I see you in bed, and looking like a good little boy with no defenses, I'm going to begin taking down those bars to a better acquaintance. May I?"

"Of course. . . . I should like nothing better. I can't put up bars now—certainly not against you, Mrs. Burns."

"You stubborn person! Won't you please let me be 'Ellen' to you?"

"If you will." The thought of it made him very happy.

"You and I haven't seen much of each other, have we? You've been far too busy, and your friendship with Red has been due to your professional contacts. I think you've got out of every invitation to our home I've ever given you." Her gay glance challenged him to deny it. He could only make a little gesture of apology. "But you've come professionally, so many times, and seen us through so many difficult, anxious days. I can never forget. Neither can Red. And now that you're having to lie by for a little, up here, I'm so anxious you shouldn't keep on worrying that Red is staying here with you, instead of being with us. The honest truth, Max . . ."

Would it do it every time—that queer pulse of his? What an odd old duffer he was that a woman couldn't speak his name without his behaving inside like a bashful schoolboy. Ah, but it was *this* woman —that made all the difference.

". . . is that you're doing me an enormous favor by letting Red stay. Though he doesn't know it, he needs the rest almost as much as you do, but he'd only take it for your sake, if he thought you needed him. So, don't you see? It's your plain ungarnished duty—didn't some poet use that phrase?—to let go and just be chums with him. I think, to look at you—though you look much better than when I saw you last—you're still not relaxing and letting this place have its chance with you. Won't you do that— for our sakes—Red's and mine?"

He lay looking at her, drinking her in. It was to him a marvelous moment, for with the question she had put out that warm, firm hand of hers and was letting it rest on his with a gentle pressure. He wanted to turn his own over and grasp hers, but . . . again he was too conscious of its chill and dampness. The sense of her affectionate touch was to this celibate almost . . . what an embrace from her might have been to Red—or to any man who loved her.

She was waiting for him to answer, and he was

slow in answering, because he knew she would then take her hand away. And then, suddenly, everything was too much for him, and he did turn his hand over and seized hers and held it, and looked for just this once into her pitiful, comprehending black eyes with all his long-suppressed worship of her showing in his own.

She gave him back the look, steadily, deeply, as though she felt it the one thing she could do for him. She put out her other hand and held his in both her own and said very gently:

"Dear Max . . . I'm so glad. Now I can go away quite happily, knowing you acknowledge the friendship with me as well as with Red. I wanted that so much. I came in here deliberately intending to break down those reserves of yours, because I was sure you needed to have them broken down. We love you so dearly. I don't mind saying that in the least, it's so true. My dear friend, promise me you'll put your own will—your magnificent will you've exercised all your life—into getting well, for our sakes."

It was almost more than he could bear, it touched him so deeply and thrilled him so poignantly. To have Ellen Burns . . . all to himself . . . for this moment.

He lost his head—at least he would have called it losing it, though any other man would have smiled at the idea—and answered hoarsely, with his eyes still searching hers: "If you'll say—for *your* sake —Ellen . . ."

"Of course I'll say it. Anything to make you do it. For my sake, then, Max. . . . And I mean it, too—*for my sake.*"

"Yes . . . I'll try." He was suddenly a little exhausted. She saw it and jumped up.

"We've been too emotional, I'm afraid, but I don't mind, if you don't. I'll get you a glass of orange juice, or something."

"I don't want it. I'm all right."

"You must have it."

She went out, and after a moment Red came in with her. Very soon he took her away. But as they went he looked back at his friend, smiling.

"She's pretty dear, eh, Max?"

Buller nodded.

"She shall be as dear to you as she likes. She's coming up for each week-end with us, and we shall have that to look forward to."

"That will be great," answered Buller, in as strong a tone as he could manage.

"Till next Saturday, then," said Ellen, with a wave of her hand.

Buller lay weakly back against his pillow. Presently, he lifted the hand she had held, looked at it, and put it to his lips. He thought he mightn't get well—he didn't know—but at least—she and Red would see him through. It was enough to go on with, since he had to go on awhile yet. And there was, all at once, something shining in the thought of going on . . . with them.

Anyhow, it was vacation time at last.

LETTER from Dr. Burns to his sister, Anne Sutherland, in a sanitarium in Southern Italy.

DEAR ANNE:

I've had a queer experience to-day, and since as I sit down to write to you I can't think of much else, I may as well let you have it. I don't know when anything has happened that got me so by the throat.

I don't know whether you remember Amy Mathewson. In the earlier days of my practice she was not only my office nurse, but she used to work opposite me at the operating table whenever I couldn't be sure of the right man. I used her for a special type of cases—I won't bother to go into that. But she was great stuff, and I prized her very highly —and was mostly in too much of a hurry to tell her so.

She left me about four years ago. She'd been taken ill while at her own home, a long way off, on a short vacation. I filled her place with considerable success—got a bright, intelligent young nurse, who wasn't Amy, by a long shot, but who made both me and my patients much more aware of her quite charming personality than Amy ever had. So when Amy wrote she couldn't come back I sent her a hasty scrawl of regret and best wishes, plus a check for her services, and went on, ungrateful and uncomprehending, man fashion, without further thought of her. Ellen, who understands quite a lot of things that I overlook, sent her a letter which was by no means a scrawl, added a good deal about how much we both thought of her, bearing heavily on my own appreciation of her and the tremendous loss I felt she would be to me, and sent her also some sort of gorgeous gift such as a woman thinks of at such times and a busy man doesn't—unless he is in love.

To-day Amy Mathewson came into my office—after four years. She didn't send in her name—asked Miss Carter to hold it back because she was an old friend and wanted to surprise me. Well—she surprised me all right.

She'd been a pretty girl of the kind that once we'd have called "modest." Nobody ever uses that word any more, probably. I mean that she was very quiet, sweet faced, soft voiced, absolutely without guile, unbelievably conscientious, faithful, loyal, self-effacing. Can you see her, even though you don't remember her? Well trained and efficient in her work, but even there never assertive—unless that became her duty, in which case she could be unexpectedly firm. In other words, she was what you would call drab—I suppose she was drab, as compared with the young woman of these days. Certainly, I never saw in her or guessed at then what I saw to-day.

To-day she wasn't drab. Yet all the color had faded from her face, she had grown very thin, her hair was beginning to show a touch of gray at the ears, she was dressed with the same careful neutrality that had always been her preference, and over her eyes she wore dark spectacles. No, mostly because of those spectacles, I didn't know her until she spoke.

"Dr. Burns, I'm Amy Mathewson."

You could have knocked me down and I wouldn't have noticed it, I was so amazed. I had to pull myself together to say that I was mighty glad to see her and wouldn't she sit down and tell me all about herself. I sat staring at her then while she explained that she had been coming through on her way

South and had stopped off to see us. Miss Carter had told her that Mrs. Burns and the children were away, but she had wanted to see me most, because she had worked for me so long, and she didn't know whether she would ever see me again because——

Anne, the dear, tired thing has had an injury to her eyes, and it's irreparable. The wrong drug shot into them by mistake. She'll be totally blind in another six months—at thirty-six. There's nothing that will stop it. She's been learning massage, because that's the one thing she could think of to do without sight. She was on her way down to a friend in Tennessee—another nurse—who will try to get such work for her. She's brave as they make 'em. No, she wouldn't stay and make us a visit, she wouldn't even stay the night—there was nothing she would let me do for her—nothing, thank you, Dr. Burns. She'd just come to——

She stood up—I stood up. Anne, I wouldn't be telling you this if I didn't think it might be good for you to hear, just now, when you feel as though you'd had rather a bad time and are more or less dissatisfied with your life anyway. Amy Mathewson is nothing to you—you'll never tell of this—Ellen's *the only other person who will hear of it, when she comes back. Just how it will touch her I know well enough. I more than suspect she always knew.*

"Dr. Burns," said this little person—she had already shown me her eyes, but she took off the spectacles again. Her eyes are still beautiful—when one doesn't look too close—"I came to tell you something because I think it will be a relief to me to do it—now. I never would have dreamed of telling you—until—I knew what was coming. I came to— look at you once more—if you wouldn't mind standing in a quite bright light. Because—I couldn't help loving you all those years I worked for you."

Anne, I swear I could have burst out crying like a schoolboy. But I didn't, though all the pity that was in me surged up in my throat till it nearly choked me. I took her hand and led her over to the brightest examining floodlight I have in the private office, turned it full on my own face, and stood there. To watch her try to get me in focus was a thing to break the heart. I thought she was never going to be able to do it, but finally I could see that she had managed it, and could see me fairly well in that terrific light that must have brought out every feature. She stood and gazed at me as long as she could bear it, and then she suddenly turned and put on the spectacles again, and I could see the tears running down her cheeks. I couldn't say a word. But she did.

"You look so little changed," she said. "I can't understand it, with your crowded life. There are lines in your face, but they don't spoil it—they only make it stronger. I—oh, you don't know how glad I am to see you again—just this once again, Dr. Burns."

I found my voice. "You're going to see me again many times, Amy dear. I've got to change those plans of yours. You're going to stay in this town —my wife and I will find you a place. We'll see you through this till you get used to it, and we'll——"

She shook her head. I knew I couldn't move her. I realized what a will had been behind all her quiet ways all her life. Somehow, for all the signs of strain and suffering in her, I suddenly saw her as a dear creature, still young—why, as young as you are, Anne—only thirty-six, and what's that, for a woman? There was something exquisite about her face, as there always had been, and as I re-membered.

"No," she said. "And I shouldn't have come if I

*hadn't known it would be the last time. Because I
had to tell you—what I have told you."*

*Modest is the word, Anne. Imagine a young
woman of these times hesitating much to let a man
know she had always thought a lot of him—more
than of any other. Why, how many women have let
me hear that, first and last, and in no uncertain
terms—just as they have any other man who happened to take their fancy. But, I tell you I understood that it was the moment of her life, to Amy
Mathewson, when she said she had always loved
me. And for all her simple way of putting it, I knew
I had actually been the passion of that poor, cir-
cumscribed life.*

*There was just one thing I could do for her, and
I did it. Took her in my arms and gave her a long
kiss—such a kiss as a man might have given her if
he had loved her as she loved him. I did it with a
will, too. I ought to have been shot if I hadn't. And
she took it like a gift from God. Perhaps it was
that, to her. I knew she'd take it with her, into the
dark, because she was like that—and because she
was starving and for once she had been fed. Just
once. My God, Anne, think of that!*

She went away without another word, and I

didn't follow her out, because I had wits enough to realize she wouldn't want me to. I sat still and thought about it, and what I thought was plenty.

I guess that's all.

Yours,
RED.

IV

I CAN'T get her to come in," explained Mr. George Graham to Dr. Redfield Pepper Burns, in his private office. "She insists on sitting in the car. I can manage"—he said it with distress in his face—"corporations, but I can't manage my daughter. I am so anxious to have you see her."

"We can bring that about. I'll go out to the car," replied Dr. Burns promptly. "As for corporations —I've always understood that compared with daughters, at almost any age—well . . . Just give me a few facts to go on, will you, Mr. Graham?"

"The one fact it is most necessary for you to know," said Mr. Graham, taking a handkerchief of extreme fineness from his breast pocket and passing it across his troubled brow, "is that she has been married and divorced twice. And she is only twenty-four."

Burns's eyebrows drew together in an odd way. Then they smoothed out again. He didn't look in the least daunted by the news.

"That does seem to be a sort of symptom," he acknowledged. "Not necessarily so serious a symptom as it would have been twenty years ago, but still—rather disturbing to a parent. What, Mr. Graham, did you feel that I could do for her? I imagine she's not physically much affected by this state of her affairs."

Mr. Graham gave him a surprised glance. "How could you guess that? She doesn't seem to be—in the least. Yet nothing can be done with her in the way of getting her to take any interest in life. That's what I'm anxious about."

"She's used up a good many of the interests, I judge," mused Burns, "that ordinarily extend over quite a term of years. Do I gather the idea that she is, in the terms of to-day, 'bored?' "

"That is her own word for it," admitted the young divorcee's father.

"I see. And you've suggested foreign travel, a long sea voyage, taking an apartment in Paris with a woman friend, going into social service work, going to bed, possibly going into your office?"

"Dr. Burns, you are possessed of powers of divination which seem most unusual. I have suggested all except the last. My daughter is hardly fitted——"

"I presume not. Suppose we go out and let her take a look at me."

"And you at her, Dr. Burns. Of course, that is what I am anxious for."

Burns opened a door out of his private office which led into his home's own hallway, thus evading patients in the waiting room. He led Mr. Graham out by this route to the street, and so to the great black motor standing well down the line of waiting cars. A chauffeur got out instantly and opened the rear door, inside which sat one who looked to Burns, approaching, like some haughty young princess refusing to see anything within her line of vision. Indeed, he said to himself, she looked even haughtier than any princess whose photograph taken at lawn parties on royal estates he had ever scanned in the illustrated edition. The case was becoming interesting. He always did enjoy meeting obstacles, and this one was very good-looking.

"Eleanora," said her father, in his gentlest tones, "Dr. Burns has been so kind as to come out himself—though he is very busy. My daughter, Dr. Burns."

Although the red-haired surgeon had saved her father's life, his daughter didn't put out her hand.

She gave him a glance and a slight nod. He returned them with a look at her which went for an instant deeper than hers at him. He gave her no word at all. He didn't even smile—since she didn't. By no possibility could she have called his manner ingratiating. He really paid her scant attention, but turned back immediately to her father. Upon which she quite naturally looked at him again. He was worth looking at, as many people before her had discovered.

"Mr. Graham," said Burns, "this is Saturday afternoon, and I'm leaving in an hour for your camp. You've never visited it since you lent it to my friend Dr. Buller. My wife and my son Bob are there to-night. I'd like them to meet you—and you them. Two other people may run up this evening. You know that cabin will easily accommodate a dozen guests, and we have an extra force in the kitchen over these week-ends. If you and your daughter will do us the honor——"

He and Mr. Graham together turned back toward Eleanora, and this time her eyes and Burns's met for a longer period than before. Now Burns had a way of looking at women, when he wished to bring them to his will, which usually accomplished that end. It was merely a perfectly steady gaze, only slightly prolonged, which had no invitation in it, but which nevertheless suggested to them that they might find him interesting to talk to. Perhaps he perfectly understood this power of his; it was more or less magnetic, yet it was still more than that. *Will you give in to me?* it seemed to say. *You're likely to be glad if you do. And you're going to, anyway.*

The young woman in the car must have felt some slight prospect of release from that boredom from which she suffered, for she now responded—in a low monotone and to her father's intense surprise: "We may as well, I suppose, since you ask us. Of course, Father's crazy to get to that camp again." She still didn't smile, and neither did Burns. It was apparently a very serious decision. Mr. George Graham glanced again at the man whom, since that affair of the life-saving operation, he considered one of the best friends he had in his full yet lonely world. Could this, he thought, be the chief of staff whom he remembered as coming in to sit by his bedside at the hospital and remain for a quarter hour of such entertaining, jolly talk as braced him tremendously—gave him the feeling of the "big man" on the job who wasn't in the least worried about him? No, there was nothing "jolly" about Dr. Burns now; he was extremely dignified.

"Then that's settled," said Burns to Graham. "I'll telephone up, and they'll be ready for us. Could you fill in the time for another hour?"

They filled it in—somehow. Burns filled his in—everyhow. Then the two motors set out together, were within sight of each other twice during the fifty miles, and arrived together at the cabin.

2

"DAD," said Bob, a few minutes later, catching his father coming out from his room, "who is she? The Queen of Mesopotamia or something?"

"The Queen of Mesopotamia," replied Red, "would be a midnight brunette. This queen is midday. Very beautiful, isn't she?"

"Well, I—yes, I think so. But she has me guessing."

"Has she, eh? Keep on guessing, and when you've guessed, let me know. It may be a help to me."

"You can fathom everybody, Dad. Fathoming implies depth, though. Maybe there isn't any, in this case."

"You surprise me. But one can't always tell."

"She'd better be nice to you," Bob asserted. "And to Mother."

"Don't worry about Mother, Bob."

"No. Naturally not. She could take care of anybody. But I don't want to have to think too badly of Queen Blonde."

"Give her a chance."

"I will. She's too stunningly pretty not to."

Burns laughed and went his way to the long central room, at one end of which a candle-lighted table was being laid for dinner. The big cabin pretended to no formality, yet bright-hued wild flowers and candles always lent a touch of civilized charm to the evening meal when Mrs. Burns was there to superintend.

3

MISS ELEANORA GRAHAM came out from her room opening on the gallery which extended the length of the cabin. She descended the staircase with its rustic railing as though she were making a stage entrance—as she virtually was, for the rest of the company awaited her. She moved slowly and languidly, her chin well up, her floating flame-and-green chiffon draperies and bared shoulders and arms suggesting that she had in her ample luggage nothing more suitable for a camp in the hills, and that, anyhow, she wouldn't have worn anything except dinner dress if she had had any amount of simpler attire to draw upon. She was delicately smoking a cigarette in a long jade holder, and her eyebrows seemed to be attempting to hold up the smooth expanse of her white forehead, from which her shining yellow hair was drawn smoothly away. Apparently she was completely surrounded by an exotic atmosphere of her own which she had brought with her.

At the foot of the stairs Bob met her in his best manner and moved beside her, a smiling young escort who had instantly whispered in her ear: "Gosh, but I'm all bowled over. Used to nothing but sun-tanned backs and arms—bruises, discoloring. How do you keep 'em that way?"

She condescended to Bob. "I'm not fond of yellow and brown—in backs."

"I'm pure bronze."

"It doesn't matter—for you. Nothing would matter—for you."

"Now, who wouldn't be flattered? I had an idea you wouldn't take the trouble for that."

"It makes a difference," she murmured. Then added languidly to Mrs. Burns as she approached the waiting group: "Sorry if I'm late."

Bob's mother was definitely a contrast to her youthful guest. She had lately come in from a scramble through the forested hills, her face, neck, and arms a peach-like tan. She had hurried glowing from her hot tub with an icy shower following, arranged her silky black hair in its usual smooth and distinguished-looking order, and slipped into a sleeveless straight silk sports frock of an apricot shade which immensely became her. Her appearance suited the cabin as the background of the cabin suited her. And her pleasantly assured speech and manner fitted herself, as always.

"You're not late, we're merely early," said Ellen. "We're always hungry, up here, and we prick up our ears at the first sound of forks and spoons being laid."

"Must be so nice to be hungry," Eleanora commented. And considered her duty done by her hostess.

At the very informal dinner she sat between Bob and some man whose personality she considered negligible. An older guest, a middle-aged woman, had the place Eleanora had expected, at Dr. Burns's right—the only seat the younger would have cared to occupy. The woman's husband, who was an African explorer of note, was ugly. Bob was a nice boy, and Eleanora gave him a little attention—all he merited. At twenty-four she had passed the stage where she could bother much with youths of seventeen when there were attractive older men present, married or unmarried. The man on her left didn't count as one of these. He happened to be a quite famous person, but she turned her shoulder upon him, since turning toward Bob brought Red into exact range. Beneath slanting lashes she kept an observant eye—also an acute ear—upon her host. *Here,* now, was a new personality, and there were always possibilities. Whenever he glanced her way —which wasn't too often—she was ready for him. She hadn't been married—and divorced—twice at twenty-four for nothing. She understood to the last flicker of an eyelid, the curve of a lip, the presentation of an alluring profile, how to engage and presently to concentrate the attention of any man upon herself. Almost any man. The one thing she didn't know was that she was to Burns no new discovery. She was an open book, and one he had often read before. The portrait of the author at the front page was pleasing, but the text . . .

However, he intended to read the text—again. There might be something he had missed. He didn't consider himself omnipotent. Neither did he feel it necessary to be blind to beauty, even though it wasn't the type to which he was most loyal. At the same time Red peculiarly enjoyed now and then playing his own professional game, which was that of keeping the upper hand of any woman, never letting her know whether she had made a palpable hit —or not—when it came to his own case.

This one, according to her watchful father's will, was Red's patient. He was in duty bound to study her. And Ellen—yes, Ellen always understood. Why shouldn't she? She was everlastingly secure, deep in his heart, and she knew it—absolutely. No surface attraction toward any younger woman—there could be none more beautiful in his eyes—could touch her. Therefore he could maneuver as he would, and by what methods, to get at all he wanted to know about this Eleanora for her anxious father's sake. Ellen would aid and abet him, smiling—bless her!

It was considerably later, and the dinner over, when there came an interruption. Eleanora had been sulking for an hour because Burns was giving all his attention—his eyes and ears and apparently every particle of his interest—to the ugly-faced explorer, who had great tales to tell to which everybody was drawn to listen absorbedly—even Bob, Eleanora forgotten. The interruption was in the usual form of a telephone call, to which Burns responded, at the far end of the room. He didn't shout, as was his custom, but kept his voice low, and as the deep-throated African traveler continued without pause in his recounting of an astounding adventure with an enraged lioness, nobody knew what Red was saying.

It was the old story. Red must be off on the instant. Those who live under the same roofs with these doctors and surgeons know that it's no joke, no fiction, these constant summonses, always at the least desired hour. Red was supposed to be out of call when up here for the week-ends, fifty miles from home, but already the village at the foot of the hills knew him. And there was a lighted landing field and fueling station for several privately owned airplanes two miles beyond the village. The men there also knew Burns well, and for good reasons.

"Mighty sorry, everybody. Must run. Crack-up at the landing field."

"Dad!" Of course it was Bob, rushing after him.

But someone else was rushing, too. Catching her flame-and-green chiffon skirts about her, Eleanora Graham had leaped out of her chair and her sulkiness at the same instant, and the quick click of her high heels sounded sharply on the cabin floor above the thud of Bob's running feet.

"Oh, Dr. Burns! Please, please take me! I must go—I must!"

Burns paused for a moment on the threshold. "No—neither of you. Or—yes! . . . Eleanora—come along!"

"Nora!" Mr. Graham stood up protestingly.

"Please let her go, sir. Dad'll look after her." Bob was smothering his own disappointment. Why couldn't Dad take them both? But if he wouldn't, there was probably a reason. Dad couldn't be—bowled over by Eleanora? No, hardly. Yet . . . A glance at his mother reassured him. She was explaining to the explorer and his wife about the landing field.

"His emergency surgical kit is always in the car," she said. "And since there's no surgeon in the little village down there, if anything goes wrong at the field when they know he's up here they always send.

He keeps his own little ship there while he's learning to fly her, and sometimes the training pilot flies him and his patient to our hospital in the city."

"His own little ship," repeated Mr. George Graham. "It can't be very small, to take several passengers. I hope—Eleanora—I hope they won't be flying in to-night."

"See here, Mr. Graham." Bob tackled him instantly and eagerly. "I don't imagine she'll get any such chance—she's much too dressed up for a trip like that. He'll leave her behind, and somebody'll bring her up. Dad ought to have let me go down with 'em—I could have brought her back in case he had to go on. But it may be nothing serious."

"I have never flown," said Mr. Graham. "Nor, to my knowledge, has my daughter. I shouldn't wish her to—certainly not at night."

"You'll have to get air-minded, sir," Bob assured him. "There's nothing like night flying."

"I imagine not. I have no wish to experience it," said Mr. Graham.

Bob went and stood in the doorway, looking wistfully down toward the landing field, the flashes of whose revolving beacon he could just make out through the trees. These old fellows, how scary they

were. Except Dad. They might not give Dad a
license on account of his age, but he was training, just
the same. He said that something might happen,
sometime, to his pilot, and then, with or without
license, it would be a mighty handy thing for him to
be able to take over the controls. As for Bob, he was
agreed with that. Gosh, but why had Dad blocked
him to-night and taken a lot of flowered chiffon with
him instead?

There was the big Graham car, and the chauffeur
smoking cigarettes outside the log-hewn garage in
a chair tipped back against it. Why shouldn't the
two of them dash down to the field, too? . . . He
was about to run out and propose this when a second
thought restrained him. Dad didn't want him
around, or he would have taken him along. . . .
Besides, there was that explorer inside, and the other
guests. He mustn't desert his mother, he supposed.
He went in. But he went out again, to look off into
the air, at least every five minutes.

4

BURNS said not a word as the car fled down the hill
and out upon the road. Eleanora also was silent. But

this was a different silence from the sulky one. She was electrically alive now, as she had not been for a long, long time, and she would have delighted to talk to the man beside her. But experience gave her her cue—don't bother a man until he shows signs of wanting to be bothered. He would show those signs, when this crisis was past, or she would have lost her bag of tricks—a beautifully embroidered bag and full to the top. She knew she had it with her. She never left it behind.

They were at the landing field in no time at all. A small crowd had collected about the damaged plane. Another group surrounded the injured flier on the ground.

"Sit still in the car till I find what's needed," Burns said, and was out and off.

He was met by a young man who reported: "We don't know what shape he's in, Doctor. It was some crash. . . ."

Eleanora sat and watched. Besides the wrecked plane there were two others in the field, one a cabin plane, the second and smaller of the open type, and in its cockpit the flier still sitting, talking quietly over its edge to a mechanic. This flier looked to Eleanora at a distance like a boy, but after a minute or two the sturdy young figure climbed out, and the pair came past Burns's car. In the night air Eleanora caught a bit of low-voiced talk. One of the voices was distinctly that of a girl, in spite of her deep, toned, throaty speech.

"I saw him taking off at Warner, and I didn't like the way his motor sounded even then. I hopped off after him. I was just playing around, anyway. I don't know why—I followed him. The whole thing happened like a flash. From the distance I was at it was hard to tell what caused it."

The mechanic answered: "He just made the field with a dead stick, and I guess that, with the lighting none too good, was too much for him. He probably hadn't had any too many hours."

"He looked awfully young to me."

"You look pretty young yourself," commented the mechanic. "But your record . . . You see I know you by your pictures."

"Oh, records—" the throaty voice sounded impatient—"they're nothing—when this sort of thing happens. If I could have done anything—but of course, I couldn't."

"Absolutely not."

The two went slowly forward toward the group

about the figure on the ground. Burns was rising from his examination as they reached him. He was giving orders to his pilot. Things were being done. Some of the onlookers, hearing, drifted over to the cabin plane, following the pilot.

Burns came over to Eleanora in the car, sitting in her flimsy evening draperies. She had just lighted a cigarette. Even in the rush to go with him she had snatched up a little glittering case which contained supplies.

"I'm taking the boy in to the hospital—in a plane," he said. "There's room for you, if you want to go. It's only twenty or twenty-five minutes to the airport."

He looked pretty grim, she thought. But if there could be any new experience for her, anywhere, she wanted to get it. She didn't see just how he could take her and a patient at the same time, but she soon found out. When she reached the cabin plane she saw that the three seats on one side of it had been converted by some mechanical device into a bed. The motor was being warmed up, with the pilot at the controls. Presently men were lifting the injured boy into the plane. When he had been placed, Burns helped Eleanora up into the middle seat on the other side and himself took the one behind her, where he was close to his patient's head, which was heavily bandaged, so that only one closed eye and a browned yet blanched cheek could be seen. She was tremendously excited, but not in the least afraid, either of the projected trip or of the still figure beside her. She was no longer smoking. Burns had made a gesture, when she first approached the plane, which had caused her to fling the cigarette away.

The girl pilot came up to the plane. "Mind if I trail you in?" she shouted to Burns, above the roaring of the motor.

"Not at all. Know him?"

She shook her head. "I saw him crash. I'd like to see how he comes out."

Burns nodded. Then he gave another order. The mechanics pulled the chocks away. The plane now taxied down the field, turned into the wind, and after a short run took off and winged away into the night. The girl pilot was up and following immediately thereafter.

5

THERE were comments from the group left behind on the ground.

"What in blazes did Doc take that fluffy dame for? About as much use as a Christmas tree in a windstorm."

"If you try to figure out why R. P. B. does *anything,* you've got another guess coming. Don't imagine he took her along for *use.*"

"Didn't know what else to do with her. *I'd* have driven her up to camp for him."

"Guess she could have driven herself. Looks like the sort that gets pulled for speeding and then gives the cop one of those smiles——"

"Suppose he'll pull the kid through?"

"Even R. P. can't do miracles. Kid looked like a goner to me. When they get a bash on the head like that——"

"Too young to be flyin', anyhow."

"No, he isn't too young, but he oughtn't to be ramming around in the dark."

"Bet he's no younger than Betty Bevan there, and she——"

"Say! That wasn't Betty Bevan!"

"You bet it was. I talked with her." This was the young mechanic whom Eleanora had noted, because he was a handsome chap, with curly hair, and though he was greasy and dirty in his mechanic's clothes, her glimpse of him in the headlights of Burns's car as he and the girl pilot had passed her had shown her how little clothes can disguise a pleasing personality.

"Well, *say!* Why didn't you tip us off?"

"Picture's been in all the papers for months. She didn't want to be introduced to this crowd."

Groans went up. The group was composed of all sorts of people, mostly men, who had rushed from neighboring farms or had stopped their automobiles in the road at the sound of the crash. A few had been already on the field: the night watchman and two or three mechanics, accustomed to look after the planes left in their charge. Not a man of them —or not more than one or two—but would rather have shaken hands with snub-nosed, wide-mouthed, tanned, yet after all highly stimulating Betty Bevan of flying fame at twenty-one than to have followed in the train of the unknown beauty in evening dress who had walked by them without looking at them on her way to Dr. Burns's cabin plane.

6

ELEANORA would have given a year of her life rather than have missed being exactly where she was on that short night flight. She had in her own way done everything there was to do in her world except fly. In other words, she had passively followed the sports, watched polo games, golf and tennis tournaments, been a member of yachting parties, driven her own powerful car. The parties had been more than the activities. Flying hadn't yet attracted her. Among her long list of men acquaintances none of them had owned or flown a plane—rather curiously, or perhaps not curiously, at all, for none of them were of the adventurous type. She had had several chances to explore the skies, but her father had suggested to her that that was the one thing he didn't wish her to do, and that if she stayed on the ground her allowance would continue to be larger than the average. She had laughed and told him that that was easy money for her: she had never yet met a man she wanted to fly with. And that was the whole point at issue with Eleanora: whatever she did must be done with an attractive man.

That condition had now been fulfilled. She was flying through the night with the most attractive man she had ever met, years older than she though he was, and apparently most satisfactorily married. These obstacles, as has been indicated, meant nothing to her. She was intensely conscious of him, behind her, his fingers on his patient's thready pulse, his whole self very evidently concentrated on the problem before him. She couldn't even imagine why he had brought her along. . . . Anyhow, she was saying to herself, he would have to bring her back, and that injured boy wouldn't be with them then. More than likely he would die before they could get him to a hospital. She couldn't, at the moment, seem to care whether he did or not. Pilots crashed every day, she knew. And she hadn't even seen his real face.

Lights far ahead, of a city. Lights of an airport, two miles outside the city.

In spite of the tragedy beside her, she hadn't been unaware of that other drama of the night flight. The moonlit fields below her, the streams in shadows, the great patches of black, the small, twinkling villages. Then, before she could realize that the journey was almost over, she was watching the strange pattern that the lights made in the city as they approached it, stretching out like a crazy quilt. Now they were beginning to come down—a sickening sensation. She couldn't see the landing field, it seemed as though they might be going to land where they shouldn't. The red lights on the tops of telephone poles, tanks, and other obstacles to be avoided—the ground itself —all seemed to be rushing up toward them. Eleanora held her breath. When they neared the ground she understood for the first time how fast they had been flying, the speed was apparently so great now in the brilliancy of the floodlights.

A mail plane had just arrived. Activity was everywhere. In no time at all they were coming down into the field, where a waiting ambulance was drawn up. Their pilot was making the smoothest landing in his power, but against the impacts of the unavoidable bumps Burns was expertly lifting and cushioning his patient's head to secure it against further concussion.

The patient safely in the ambulance, Burns turned to Eleanora. "Will you go to the hospital with us or wait here?"

"I'll go, please."

Eleanora was aware that the men on the field supposed her to be the wife or friend of the unconscious pilot. The young hospital interne who had come with the ambulance gave way without apparent surprise when Burns said: "Let us have the two inside seats, will you, Doctor?" and motioned Eleanora up to sit on the leather seat beside the stretcher with him. She was beginning to have a strange feeling that she *was* after all, and in spite of herself, somehow concerned with that inert figure. Yet the whole thing was impossible. She had never been in an ambulance in her life, had never even looked inside of one. She was accustomed to send flowers to hospitals but not to visit them. Dressed in her gay chiffons, a flame-colored evening wrap over her bare shoulders and arms, long earrings dangling from her small ears, she felt suddenly unreal beside all this stark reality of injury and helplessness and possible deep tragedy.

How old was that boy beside her? Certainly no older than she, and probably life was all over for him. And here was this doctor beside her, absorbedly concerned with whether the boy lived or died, though he had never seen him before, any more than she.

Not noticing her for a moment. Yet why had he brought her along? That was the question which kept coming uppermost. Certainly, it must be an unusual thing to do, in such a case.

They reached the hospital. She heard Burns's low-voiced orders.

"Not a jar—take it slowly—very slowly. No—not to the operating room. To the third elevator. . . . Easy—easy. . . ."

The young hospital interne was at Eleanora's side. It looked as though Dr. Burns had forgotten her. Dr. Ingram knew he undoubtedly had. All right, let him look after the patient himself, if he preferred; the interne would be delighted to attend to this by now slightly disheveled but exquisite passenger. Burns had left the plane windows open; Eleanora's fair waves had been blown about, but Ingram liked them that way. Her eyes hadn't followed the stretcher bearers, he wasn't sure that she was as anxious as she had a right to be if the patient were anything to her. Ingram knew just about what that type of bandaging indicated—a blow—probably a fracture—at the base of the skull. If so, not much use operating—if the boy were fit for it, which the orders given indicated that he was not. Too much shock, undoubtedly. . . . Well, Ingram was glad not to have any responsibility in the case himself. Sometimes things happened less opportunely than this arrival at the hospital with a distinguished surgeon in charge and ready to dispense with internes. A clinic was a clinic, and the internes and others were expected to be present: but Burns wasn't accustomed to call in mere observers when things were urgent in an emergency. Ingram didn't think he himself stood particularly high with Dr. Burns. Ingram had—made a few mistakes in the past which Burns had found it hard to overlook. . . . They had been avoidable mistakes—made from negligence.

But Ingram didn't neglect Eleanora. He escorted her to a big, dimly lighted waiting room, a comfortable place, where anxious friends of patients were apt not to notice the rugs and divans and pictures on the walls. At this hour of the evening—it was now ten o'clock—there was nobody there. He seated Eleanora and took a chair near her. He felt this an opportunity not to be lost. And then, just as they had exchanged a few words, somebody was coming in. It was the sturdy girl pilot of the first landing field, her helmet off, her thick brown hair more

ruffled than Eleanora's. Eleanora's wasn't ruffled
now, anyway; she had caught sight of herself in a
mirror and had quickly run ordering fingers over her
head.

The girl walked straight over to the young doctor,
who rose reluctantly to meet her. He preferred
chiffons to leather, anytime.

"Are you Dr. Ingram, please?"

"I am."

"How is he, please?"

"Who—please?"

"The patient just brought in from the plane."

"Suffering from shock, naturally."

"Isn't his skull fractured?"

"Really I—we don't give out information before
we have any."

Betty Bevan looked at him rather hard. Then she
glanced at Eleanora, whom she seemed not to have
seen before.

"I'm sorry," she said, at once. "I didn't realize
you were the one who came over with Dr. Burns. I
just asked for information at the office, and they
sent me up here. They said Dr. Ingram would know
about the flier. May I wait here—at the other end
of the room?"

"Certainly," Ingram responded for Eleanora, who was staring at Betty Bevan. This girl interested her. She had never seen any girl like her. She was not often interested in anyone of her own sex, but Miss Bevan possessed a drawing power all her own.

Then suddenly Ingram himself recognized her. That face—why, of course. Hadn't it been pictured a hundred times, in all the papers? Its owner had already made a reputation as one of the most daring yet level headed of all the young women who had gone in for aviation. Hadn't he heard that peculiar boyish voice of hers over the radio, saying a few words of gay yet modest greeting to the millions of listeners-in who had been interested in her latest exploit? Why, she had flown higher . . .

He became deferential. He might prefer chiffons to leather, but this especial wearer of leather was not one to be ignored.

"I seem to know you," he said very pleasantly. "You are—Miss Bevan, of the upper airways. Congratulations, if I may."

"Oh, thanks," responded Miss Bevan. "Then would you mind finding out more for me about the case? They must know something by now."

7

HE WENT away and left the two together. Eleanora sat still, watching the girl, who roamed restlessly about, never looking her way. Finally Eleanora, from sheer curiosity, spoke.

"Will you excuse me for asking if the young man Dr. Burns brought over from the landing field is—a friend of yours?"

Betty Bevan paused. "No—except as we all of us in the air are friends. I never saw him before. But I thought you must have."

"No. Dr. Burns merely brought me along because I happened to be with him. Would you—mind telling me something about your experience in flying?"

Betty Bevan gazed straight at the questioner. Her dark eyebrows were heavy, they nearly met above her steady brown eyes. The effect when she looked at you was one which suggested considerable force of personality. You couldn't imagine her in chiffons, even though you knew that she probably possessed evening clothes of entire suitability. There was nothing rough or untutored about her; she might have come from anywhere that was a good place to come from.

"Of course I wouldn't mind," she responded. "Only—I couldn't be specially interested to talk much about it until I know how things are going here. . . . There isn't much to tell, anyway. It's really awfully simple. Anybody can fly. Or—nearly anybody."

She walked over to the doorway and looked down the long, white-walled corridor. She had already done this several times. The corridor was empty. The hospital at this point on the lower floor, at this hour, was as quiet as a church. She turned back into the room.

"I can't quite believe that," persisted Eleanora, who was used to making people talk when she wished to know what they could tell her. "Do you think I could fly, for instance?"

Miss Bevan again seemed to study her. "Of course, the way you are dressed just now doesn't suggest it," she replied frankly. "But I ought to be able to discount that. Do you care to tell me how old you are?"

"I'm twenty-four." Eleanora felt herself obliged to tell the truth. Since her second divorce and her resumption of her maiden name she had been stand-

ing still in the matter of birthdays, as far as her
own thought of herself went.

"Well, that's young enough. I couldn't have
guessed, or I wouldn't have asked, you know. Probably you could pass the physical tests. You look perfectly well, and I imagine you have a steady hand on
a driving wheel and step on the gas when you're far
enough away from a traffic officer. It's easy enough
to find out whether you would develop what's called
flying sense, which is what you must have to make
a pilot. There are plenty of places where students can
train."

She walked away again, over to that door. This
time she met Dr. Ingram. He was looking sober
enough, at last.

"Well?"

"Dr. Burns says he hasn't a chance. He's prac-
tically going out now."

"Please take me to him."

Ingram put up a hand as if to hold her back. She
was standing straight as a young pine tree, and looking him in the eye.

"You know him personally?" he questioned.

"No. But nobody else does, either. I'd like to
stay with him."

"He hasn't recovered consciousness since his

crash. He won't. You can't do him any good. Why should you———"

"Because I'd like to. There's no rule against it, is there?"

"I suppose not. But Dr. Burns is with him, and he'll undoubtedly stay till it's over. You don't need . . . for an entire stranger . . ."

"Will you please take me to him?"

Ingram's shoulders shrugged. "Oh, certainly," he agreed. "I understand. If it's a matter of professional etiquette—one flier toward another . . ."

"Etiquette!" said Betty Bevan, in a suppressed voice of wrath.

She went out of the door, past him, and he was obliged to follow. He glanced back at Eleanora as he went. "I'm sorry," he said. "This seems to be necessary. But I'll be back at once."

Eleanora stood up. She hesitated a moment. Then she came after the others, catching up with them. "I'd like to come too," she said.

They both turned in amazement. The interne in his white hospital uniform, the girl flier in her brown suit and high laced boots, looked at this person whose appearance suggested drawing rooms or lawn parties and nothing more important.

"Don't think of it," said Ingram.

But Miss Bevan made a gesture of assent, without speaking.

Ingram led the way. He was almost guilty of shrugging his shoulders again, but refrained. People visiting hospitals always lost their heads, he was thinking. And just how Dr. Burns was going to take this visitation couldn't be foreseen. Probably he himself would come in for some blame about it.

Burns, as he sat beside the bedside in the small private room to which he had had his patient taken, did not look up as the three figures stole in. He was watching the last flickerings of what had been so shortly before an ardent flame; marking the almost imperceptible pulsations which only trained senses could still discover. His grave face was as intent as though there were anything left to do for this boy before him except to see him through.

A nurse, on the other side of the bed, stood motionless, but she did look up. She had been told that the crushed flier's identity was unknown, and that therefore nobody could be sent for. This, she understood, was why Dr. Burns himself would not turn the patient over to the hospital and go away: that wouldn't be like him.

Then, suddenly, here were Dr. Ingram and two strange girls. The interne remained beside the door when he had closed it. The fair-haired young woman in striking evening dress stayed at his elbow, her eyes widening and darkening as she stared at the austere scene before her. But the other girl, seeming like another boy in her flier's outfit, her dark brows drawn together in an expression of deep pity, went forward to the bedside opposite Burns. She stood motionless for several minutes, looking at the helpless form, studying what could be seen of the ashen young face. Then she slowly slipped down to her knees, and leaning forward put out her firm, tanned hand and very gently took hold of the hard yet flaccid one lying upon the smooth white sheet. It was easy to see that she gradually tightened her grasp. Thus she remained, without stirring, as if, having made the contact, she were trying to convey past the unconscious senses of the dying boy something which might somehow support him. Burns, now entirely aware of her presence, bestowed upon her a glance which—though she did not see it—testified to a recognition of her motive. It was his motive, too. What difference that the boy couldn't know?

So they all waited until the end, not moving.

It was a matter of perhaps fifteen minutes. During that time Eleanora's half frightened yet watchful gaze alternated between Burns himself and the kneeling girl, whose eyes never left the boy's face. Eleanora had never before been present at such a scene. If she had wished for new experience, she was having it, and it was a strange one. Two people, Dr. Burns and Betty Bevan, unacquainted with each other, were giving to an entire stranger, unconscious of their existence, something as vital as it was intangible; it represented, vicariously, that which those who knew and loved him might have given if they had been there. If not of grief like theirs, certainly of compassion and of comradeship. These two were not letting him go upon his last journey unaccompanied to his "take-off" by friends. . . .

8

ELEANORA and Betty Bevan were left alone together again in the waiting room for a few minutes while Burns and Ingram made arrangements. The two young women would be separated soon at the airport outside the city, it was not likely that they would meet again.

There was something new in Eleanora's manner. There was an eagerness in it, a willingness to make advances to another of her own sex hitherto almost entirely absent from her custom.

"Miss Bevan—will you mind if I say that I should like so much to really know you?"

"That's very nice of you. But I can't imagine why. I lead a very different life from yours, I'm quite sure. There's not much room in it for anything except this wild passion of mine for adventuring."

"But I want adventure, too."

"My sort?"

"I've tried most other kinds," said Eleanora quite simply. "They don't satisfy me. I—I'm—it seems as though I were through with everything that can interest me."

"Of course you're not—at your age."

"But I am. You don't know, and of course I can't tell you. But—I'd like to learn to do something that would give me what you have. I can't explain it— but—I never in the world would have thought of doing such a thing as you did to-night. You've no idea at all what an impression that made on me."

For a moment the girl flier regarded Eleanora as

though she didn't know quite what she meant. Then she said, with a change of tone: "Oh—*that?*"

"Yes. You didn't even know him."

"It made no difference. It made it all the more something I wanted to do. It was so little, anyway."

"I couldn't have done it."

"Then," said Betty Bevan, with that straight and searching look of hers, "I'd say you'd better learn to fly. It will give you something you need. Everybody needs it. I'm only just trying to get it."

"What is it?"

"Courage for facing things—the unknown."

9

BURNS and Eleanora and their pilot flew back to the small landing field below the Graham cabin in absolute silence. Eleanora had watched the way Burns had said good-bye to Betty Bevan as she stood by her plane; had heard what he said to her as he grasped her hand for a minute while he spoke.

"You're great stuff, Miss Bevan. I don't need the knowledge of your flying record to tell me that."

There were both admiration and respect in his eyes, as well as a strong friendliness. Suddenly

Eleanora realized that such a little speech from him must be worth more to a woman, young or old, than all the pretty compliments he might pay—if he did pay compliments, which she doubted. Nobody had ever said anything like that to *her*—nobody ever would, unless she earned it by being and doing something very different from anything she had ever been or done.

Betty Bevan smiled. "I don't need the knowledge of *any* of your records to tell me that about you, Dr. Burns," she answered.

Then she climbed into her plane. Burns and Eleanora didn't even see her full-face again, until all the preliminaries were over, and the engine warmed. As the mechanic pulled the chocks from under the wheels and the flier slowly opened her throttle, she gave one glance over the side. She taxied her plane into the wind, thereby changing her position as regarded her two new acquaintances: she was ready to roar away. Her brown, engaging young face, as she threw back at them one last clear-eyed look, was almost stern with concentration. But somehow there was in it something so alert, so coolly capable, it left with them the sense of a youthful conqueror who belonged in great and remote spaces where they would like to follow. Yet she was just a girl!

Eleanora felt very small indeed during the silent flight back and as, after the landing, she followed Burns to his waiting car. She had never known before what it could be to feel small beside any other human being. She heard him briefly answering a low question from one of the two men lingering at midnight on the field, the night watchman and the curly-haired young mechanic. It was the latter who asked:

"Any chance, Doctor?"

"All over."

A murmur of "Too bad."

That was all. Evidently, Eleanora thought, speech was not ready on such occasions. But they were sorry, she could see by their faces.

10

OFF in the car, with only two swiftly-to-be-covered miles left in which she would be alone with him, Eleanora almost instantly burst out:

"Could you—would you—go slowly? Would you —park the car for five minutes? I must talk to you, Dr. Burns. I mayn't have another chance."

He instantly slowed down, turned the car to the side of the road, and stopped it. He knew well enough that something had happened to Eleanora. He had seen it already. If she were ready to tell it to him, he must listen, no matter what the hour. It was his job.

"Dr. Burns—I think you won't believe it—but—I want to learn to fly."

"I believe it. But I want to know why, if you will tell me."

"I want to escape—from the world I know. I'm so tired of it. That girl flier——"

"Yes. She got me, too. She'd get anybody—and not know she'd done it."

"I—envied her so I could hardly bear it," said Eleanora, with a sigh. She wasn't acting now, Burns was pretty sure. She couldn't act—not after meeting Betty Bevan. Meeting her was like having breathed deeply of fresh, briskly blowing winds after having been confined in hot, vitiated rooms.

"She's someone to envy," agreed Burns. He smiled in the darkness, and Eleanora could hear the smile in his voice as he added: "I'll wager those pretty clothes you have on have bothered your thoughts ever since you got to that hospital."

How could he have guessed that?

"I hate them," agreed Eleanora between her teeth.

"I'm delighted to hear it. And I've no objection to pretty clothes, either."

"She said I could learn to fly."

"She ought to be able to size you up. I think you could, myself."

"Why do you think so?" demanded Eleanora quickly.

"Several reasons."

"Please tell me."

"I should have to be cruelly frank," admitted Burns.

"I don't mind—really I don't."

"Very well, I'll take you at your word. . . . Thus far in your life you have had your own way."

"Father's been talking to you about me."

"Certainly. I'm a physician, and he's been anxious about you."

"Well—I knew he had. Never mind—I want to know why you think I could fly."

"You've had your own way. That means that you have certain qualities not entirely to be discounted. You can put things through, in spite of opposition. Of course, your father's done that, all his life, to be where he is. And though you have had your own way you are not completely spoiled—yet. You came into that hospital room to-night. Was it entirely out of curiosity? Will you be absolutely honest in your answer to that?"

Eleanora considered. No use being anything but honest with this man. She tried to put together her own motives in insisting on following Betty Bevan and the interne to see the young flier die. One came uppermost, and it seemed to her the real one. But if she really were to be honest she must admit another, first.

"I think," she said slowly, "it must have been part curiosity, yet not altogether, because I've never wanted to see anything like that. If it was curiosity —partly—that was because I wanted to see what you were doing. Of course, your ways interest me. They are something new to me. But more than that —I liked that girl—she fascinated me. I would have gone straight up into the air with her, even if I hadn't heard that she was famous for her flying. So—when she seemed to think she must go to that room, I had the impulse to go too, just to do what she did, because it must be what ought to be done in the circumstances. . . . I know this sounds all mixed up," she ended a little breathlessly.

"Not so much mixed up but that I think I can disentangle it," Burns assured her. His voice sounded less curt, warmer, than she had yet heard it when he was speaking to her. "In other words—if you'll let me say it—for nearly the first time in your life, perhaps, you were forced to recognize in another woman attributes that were strange to you—and immensely desirable. They had nothing to do with beauty of face, or style of dress, or social position, or with anything in your world. You had met a really strong, interesting character, different in every way from anyone you had known, in a person even younger than yourself. . . . You know—" he broke off suddenly and waited a moment before he went on, in a curiously altered tone—"when she went down on her knees by that boy and held his hand— for his absent mother, or his sister, or perhaps his sweetheart, as we know she did, it touched me tremendously. She didn't do it sentimentally, she didn't cry over him, she did it in precisely the spirit in which she would have rescued him from his crash had she been able. People say the things girls and women are learning to do—particularly flying—

make them hard-boiled—take away their femininity. That didn't look like it, did it? And putting a touch of the male into the make-up of some of them is a mighty good thing. A mighty good thing it would be for you, too."

She stared at him in the darkness. She could just see the firm outlines of his profile as he looked straight ahead of him into the shadows.

"I think it would," she breathed. "I seem to be, all at once, terribly tired of—of———"

"Being all female and just playing with men?"

It was a stiff question, but she answered it.

"Yes. I think I'd rather—try being friends with them."

"That," said Burns on a whimsical note, "sounds to me a little like the declaration of the overfed lioness that she will eat no more flesh. But—I really think you might find, after all, that you didn't want any more for a while. You might get to enjoy some other kind of food. We'll have to leave that analogy—the lioness doesn't enjoy any other kind of food. But you're young, and you're physically fit, I should say. I'd like to see you substitute a really thrilling piece of work for play that's lost its thrills —in the sense that you young people use that word to-day. And of course Betty Bevan knows much more about genuine thrills than you, with all your experience. Hers mean something. The work she's doing adds considerable to the promotion of aviation and to its possibilities. In this age that's something that has to be done, by somebody."

"Will you," said Eleanora Graham, sitting upright and speaking in a tone he hardly knew for that of the young person of only a few hours before, "have it out with my father?"

"No. Oh, no!" replied Burns, with an enjoying laugh, soberly though he had been speaking a moment before. "Having it out with your father must be your first endurance test. He'll go straight up into the air and probably off into space. You'll have to follow him in a fast pursuit plane, with a machine gun, and bring him down. The endurance will come in, in the length of time it takes to overtake him without a chance to refuel by way of coming to me for support. Only when it's all over will I support you."

"But you will then?"

"Yes, I will then," promised the red-headed doctor. And put his foot upon the starter.

She might not go through with it. But he had a

strong feeling that she would. After all, she was her father's daughter.

Though, he supposed, George Graham's anxieties concerning his daughter would, when he heard of this new development, seem but to have just begun, to Red himself they would virtually seem ended.

Anxieties, that is, that really matter.

LETTER from Dr. Burns to his sister, Anne Sutherland, in a sanitarium in Southern Italy.

DEAR ANNE:

Evidently you are doing a lot of thinking, marooned there in your bed. The visits of your handsome Italian doctor don't last long at their longest, and, after all, you can't expect a doctor of any nationality to spend much of his time on any one of his women patients, no matter how pretty—and you are pretty, Anne, as you like to be assured every so often. Well, I swear you are—if you just keep down your weight. How about those chocolates? I sometimes think the devil himself invented them. He doesn't touch them himself—a fat devil couldn't get anywhere in diabolic functioning. Think that over. His Majesty is slim as an arrow, if you remember all the portraits of him by all the artists to whom he ever—stood.

But what are all these maunderings about divorce? Of course you don't mean a word of them. You couldn't really get along without Dick any more than he could without you. But, on my word, Anne, if you two go on for many more years without any aim in life except your own amusement, you're going to come to a place where the road is marked with a large sign—Dead End. Just beyond lies a big field with the grass well trodden down, and the name of it is Divorce. It's full of these free spirits who have climbed over the bars—and they're not half as free as they were before, and they're still more dissatisfied. They get out on the road again, maybe, but fairly soon there's another Dead End. And then what?

I don't mean I'm all against divorce. In certain cases it may be the only thing possible. But I don't think so in your case, and I'd be worried about you if I weren't certain you're just playing with the thought. See here, Anne. Remember Mother and Dad? Of course you do—neither you nor I could ever forget them. They had things hard almost all the years of their lives, but my Lord, how those years did knit them together! They got hold of something that saw them through, and it was worth getting. Sometimes I think the modern cynical attitude toward marriage would never exist if it weren't talked about and written about so much. People in-

fect one another with it. I read an article the other
day written by a woman who was so sorry for herself that she was enjoying herself hugely in being
just as hard and bitter as she could make herself be,
in print. She'd had too many children—three was
the awful number—her husband had earned too little
money, she hadn't had the fun she'd expected, she
never was going to have it, marriage and children
were a horrible mistake, and so on. Apparently she
hadn't had a happy moment since the first of those
children was born. The whole article was one
hysterical shriek. And it was handed me to read by
a young mother with two children with whom she'd
been immensely pleased—until she read what the
other woman had written. Instantly the germ of dis-
content was planted. She too began to feel abused
and cheated. "Cheated"—that was the writer's in-
furiated word for what had happened to her. A hard
word to have to use of oneself. But how tremendous
is the power of suggestion! The writer not only felt
cheated, herself, but she'd made the other woman
feel that way as well. Now, I ask you, what was the
good of that?

I go into my hospital at midnight and look in on
those of my patients who aren't sleeping, because of

pain, or nervousness, or for any other reason. I can leave them feeling "cheated," or I can leave them feeling soothed and hopeful. When I come in I may be more or less heavy of spirit myself, tired, perhaps, or worried. Have I a right to take it out on those people? I haven't. I have no possible right to try to make them feel worse than they did before —I have an obligation to cheer them if I can. Shall I not be honest—all our writers and speakers are being honest, these days—it is the fashion, even though it involves being brutal—shall I not be honest? I swear I won't be, if I'm going to take away the last grain of a fellow human being's courage.

I hope all goes well with you, my dear.

RED.

V

Red, I've a problem to present to you. Quite a serious problem."

"All right, Len. Let's have it."

Red and Ellen had started upon a walk over a trail through the heavily wooded hills which surrounded the Graham camp. After a quarter mile, during which not much had been said, Ellen had suddenly turned toward her husband and put her hand upon his arm. She looked up at him, meeting a gaze which seemed more than ordinarily intent. It was as though he had been waiting for her to speak, upon some subject which had been uppermost in both their thoughts, but any discussion of which he felt must be begun by her.

How glorious she was to look at, he said to himself, with her fresh hues of flushed tan, her black hair clinging tight and smooth to her small, shapely head. Her whole appearance, in her rough-and-ready sports clothes of brown and orange, was of being alive and unworn. Would she never even begin to grow old, he wondered. Not for a long time yet, if she kept herself as fit as that. She was as lithe and graceful as she had ever been. As for those black eyes of hers . . . he had never seen any quite like them. Hers was not the carefully preserved youth dependent upon artifice; it was the full flowing blood stream of perfect health and ever deepening interest in life.

"Shall we sit down? This narrow trail—I can't talk to you over my shoulder."

"Try this log. I'll sit beside you and whittle a stick. Concentrate better on problems that way. I have an idea—a sort of an idea—what this one may be."

"I imagine you have, Red dear."

He found the stick, after some search—an inviting small branch of white birch. He didn't sit down beside her, however, but took up a position astride a small stump, opposite her. She began at once, in the low-pitched voice of mellow cadences which was one of her great assets. He had often wondered why certain other women, listening to it, didn't realize how harsh or strident or shrill their own voices were by comparison.

She began without preamble. Not much use had Red for preambles, anyhow.

"It's Max. I've thought, so far, that I could keep the relation between us in complete control, just as you and I both expected it to be. But, in the last few days—it's getting a little out of hand. He's like —well—I keep thinking of someone in prison— who's always been in prison—and who's having his first look out, with a prospect of release. Can he be blamed if he begins to go—a little mad?"

"Len! Do you mean that? *Is* he? About you?"

"Yes. And I thought it was only fair to you to let you know."

If there were any whittling of that stick to be done, it would have to be by other hands. It would be a shorter stick, too, for Red had suddenly broken it in two. He leaned forward, studying Ellen's face.

"Tell me all there is."

"That's what I want to do. I must. . . . Red, there was never a stranger situation. It's not the usual one at all—the one we're all so familiar with."

"Isn't it? . . . Go on."

"I've tried so hard to be just a friend—the same kind of friend he's been to us all these years. I wanted to make him feel that he could depend upon our friendship as we have on his. You wanted to do that for him, too."

"Yes—of course. . . . That is . . ."

"He's seemed so pitiful. He's been so self-contained—almost humble—as though we were feeding a famishing dog, yet a dog that wouldn't leap at a bone till you gave the word. All these talks we've had—all these hours we've spent together—why, it was just Maxwell Buller, who would take exactly what was given him and not ask for more. . . . But now—he——"

"He's asked for more?" There was a curious, repressed note in Red's voice which showed that he was not likely to be easy on his old friend if he should ask even a little too much of Ellen.

"I think he's tried very hard, Red, not to. But because he's been happier he's certainly been growing a little stronger—eating a little better—showing more signs of not meaning to give up the fight. You know that was what I first begged of him, for our sakes. Finally—because he insisted on my putting it that way—for mine. I told you that. I told you all I said to him about our love for him. It was—I felt it then—like throwing a rope to a drowning man. I would have said anything to him that would have made him grasp at life again. You can understand that, Red. How many women, young and old, in your practise, have you pulled through because you made them feel your special interest in them?"

"Interest—of course. I never made love to them to do it." Red's hazel eyes were glowing fiercely beneath his heavy eyebrows.

Ellen looked at him, a faint incredulous smile touching her lips. He winced a little under it.

"Oh, well," he said, with some impatience, "we don't have to go into that. In a sense every successful doctor more or less has to show a sort of friendly affection for certain patients. You know well enough nothing of that sort can possibly touch *you*—you've always understood."

"Yes," said Ellen gently, "I've always understood. You have something about you that attracts people to you very strongly, both men and women. It's a type of virility which fascinates and holds them. You've used it—with my blessing, because I wasn't afraid for myself. Without it you could never have done what you have done. But—just now—if you want your friend Max to get well, you'll have to be as generous as I've been all these years."

"But you tell me yourself the situation's getting

out of hand. If that means you have to kiss the fellow good-night and good-morning—well—damn him—he'll have to get well without that. I didn't suppose——"

"Red!" Her tone was still gentle, but it was also spirited. "The situation isn't quite like that."

"Worse, then. It's getting very subtle, I suppose."

He was jealous—jealous as a Turk, as his friends had often told him—concerning Ellen. He always had been. But he had been so sure of her, he had mostly kept from showing it. Now, he said to himself, here was something new and dangerous. Before she knew it she might . . .

Max Buller wasn't in the least like Red. Red hadn't known, for instance, what a passion Max had for books of an entirely different sort from those Red himself enjoyed. That had come out when Ellen had begun to read aloud to the invalid, as she had been doing, by the hour. Red had picked up some of the books, then had taken special notice of them, as the readings went on. They weren't books of travel, exploration, adventure, such as Red himself enjoyed. They were biographies, of peculiar people—people who were to Red morbid people—geniuses propped up in sick beds; prisoners on far-off islands;

medical men who labored among lepers, themselves tainted with disease; Negroes who had lifted their heads above their kind and said or sung strange, broken-hearted yet defiant things. There had been many books of poetry, most of it melancholy, according to Red's ideas, who had flipped some of the pages and wondered if the poets wrote that way because they were really so sad or because they revelled in their sadness. For himself, he would have liked to knock their heads together and tell them to brace up. Altogether, to him, it was as though Max, ill, had become morbid too. He was delving in dark places—or so they seemed to Red, who preferred the sunlight. And Ellen was delving with him. He didn't like it. Why couldn't she read jolly sea yarns to him—or, if he must have poetry, sturdy stuff that would make him feel like getting up and facing the world again? Red supposed there must be a few people who, though they wrote verse, didn't sit on tombstones to do it.

There was another complication: Max wasn't bad-looking. Red had always thought of him as plain, almost ugly; certainly unattractive to women. But now, it had struck Red several times, as he saw Max lying in his deck chair watching Ellen as she read, that there was a certain shadowy sort of charm in the thin features and deep-set eyes which might conceivably be more appealing to her than any amount of rugged male beauty, secure in fine health and shouting all over the place, as he supposed he did, himself. That poetry reading . . . Red, who had no use for any of it, and never had considered its possible effect on lovers of it—especially on lovers of it who read it together—now found himself deeply distrusting it, all of it! Even Kipling, some of whose lusty lyrics he had happened to read when Bob had put them before him, and whom he had thought of as one sane person. Yet hadn't Bob gone around quoting a sinister line:

"And he learned about women from *her!*"

In a long professional experience, Max Buller had had every opportunity to learn about women. If he hadn't done it, Red, his best friend though he was, wouldn't have him learning about them from Ellen, not if he had to put a bullet through him. Red was well aware that he would be quite capable of that, in spite of all the years during which he had learned to keep a close and mostly successful hold upon a fiery temper which had, especially in his early years of practise, almost been his undoing.

2

ELLEN had said nothing at all since Red's use of the word "subtle" as representing the state of things between herself and Max Buller. She had sat looking off down the leafy trail up which the two had come, where big boulders on either side, hung with ferns in all the crevices, made a sort of winding alley through the trees. There was a little frown between her exquisite eyebrows; her lips were pressed together as they seldom were, as though she were exercising some self-control of her own.

"Well?" Red couldn't stand her silence any longer.

She looked up, meeting his eyes.

"I think, dear, you'll just have to take your choice between slaying your best friend by your own hand——"

Red experienced a strange jolt of his suddenly racing heart. Hadn't he been imaging, just a moment before, something like that? . . .

"—or trusting me enough to let me manage him

until he's well—if he is going to get well. He certainly won't if you—take him away from me now."

"My God!" said Red, and the hot color mounted in his face.

"I know," said Ellen, fully recognizing the violence of his reaction to her putting of the case. "You wouldn't be you if you didn't feel like that. But that's the problem, and we have to face it. The whole thing seems to be that he must have something in the world to live for, if he is to live. He has nobody——"

"Hundreds of patients—friends—as many as any of us."

"You know that isn't true, Red. He has had hundreds of patients, who were grateful for a few days and then promptly forgot him, because there seemed to be nothing about him to make them remember him forever, as your patients do you. As for friends —he says himself you are the only one. You yourself have complained time and again that in spite of the way you have tried to put him forward and have backed him up, the other doctors never show him any special honor, no matter how he's deserved it. He's been tried and true—and drably neutral, as far as anybody could see, like his surroundings,

that drab house he's lived in, and his offices, all
dun color. People haven't known him—haven't tried
to. But . . . beneath all that drabness, fires glow
—only he's been keeping them smothered, and nobody has even noticed the smoke."

"Now, see here, Len." Red's eyes were gleaming
dangerously. He was all but glaring at her, he, Red,
who worshiped her. Which, of course, was why he
was glaring. "Am I to understand he's showing
these fires to you? Fires!—Max Buller! The old
watchdog—the sick old dog who crawls and licks
your hand. Do you mean to say he's sitting up and
begging you for his life—barking at you—getting
up spirit enough to dash at you—and then lying
down again with his nose between his paws and pretending to be asleep when I come around? . . ."

Ellen got up and slowly walked away from him
down the rocky, ferny trail. Her head was proudly
up, as he had seen it many times. It was no use—
he never got anywhere with her by thundering at
her. He couldn't intimidate her. The more he lost
his temper the less headway he could make with her.
He watched her now with a sinking heart, because
he could never bear to have her turn away from him
like that on account of his own inability to be reason-

able. Yet—Lord, did she expect him to be reasonable over this thing? It had been well enough for her to show Max her charming friendliness—Red was used to seeing men irresistibly attracted to her by that, as well as by her beauty of face and person —but if it had come to talk of hidden fires springing up in this sick man's hollow breast which might burn both him and her . . . all three of them . . .

He came after her with long strides. He could no more help doing that than he could stop the pounding of his heart by laying his hand over it. Jealous . . . jealous. . . . Many times before, without reason. This time, with reason, whether she herself knew or would acknowledge it or not. Sick men—the maternal instinct in women—a thin, wistful face—imploring eyes—books of poetry— *poetry*. . . . He couldn't get to her fast enough.

"Listen to me, Len. . . . I'll try to see this thing through and trust you. I guess I've got to—you won't let go of the case now you've taken hold. I suppose I ought to understand that—I'm like that myself. But—what gets me is——"

She turned around and faced him. Her eyes searched his.

He took her face between his hot hands and

tipped her head back, looking into her eyes as though he would look her through and through. Slowly he shook his head.

"It's queer," he whispered. "There's a sort of sinking feeling at my heart I've never had before. Not even when I'd lost a case I'd fought for. It's just plain—fear."

"No, Red!"

"Yes. Something's happened at last to come between us. Maybe you don't know it yet or recognize the symptoms. I do. . . . I can put it in one word. . . . It's that damned poetry! You can laugh."

She didn't laugh. Instead she put her hand inside his coat, against his breast, where she could feel the agonized pumping of that suspicious heart. She held her warm palm there while he waited, breathing heavily. . . . Did it miss a beat, or was it her imagination? . . . Finally she took his big, shapely surgeon's hand in hers.

"Come, dear," she said. "Let's walk along the trail and find another place to sit. I want you to let me talk to you almost more frankly than I ever did before. And I want you to listen."

They had gone ten slow paces and around a bend when they came to a low, flat boulder. She drew him down beside her. His face was a little white now, under all his usual warm color.

"I'm listening," he said, and looked away.

3

"I WANT you to try to understand," she began, "even though what I'm going to say may be so far away from your own experience or conception of another person's experience that sympathy with it will be difficult."

His turned-away profile indicated this. That obstinate chin of his looked like an almost complete barrier to comprehension, although the fine outline of his nose and lips did suggest a certain sensitive-ness—if one could get past the chin!

"There's no getting around the fact," she said clearly, "that I've been enjoying these talks and readings with Max. Apart from my pity for him, I find him much more interesting than I could have imagined. He has a keen mind, and he appreciates beauty . . ."

A low growl came from Red's throat—which he immediately cleared, as though to cover that involuntary response to the word.

". . . of thought—and of word and phrase. He's had no time—all these years of hard work and scientific study—to enjoy the books he's been wanting to read. It's quite naturally a pleasure to me to give him pleasure, in such an innocent way. But of course—I recognize what you do. It's dangerous ground, I'm sure—not so much for me, as you think, as for him. Yet—he's getting well on it . . . Red, can we take the incentive away from him? You can't --you surely can't—*really* think . . ."

"I think these things are insidious," he muttered. "You know they are."

"And you can't risk my having any other friend than you?"

She had never said just that to him before. He wheeled about upon the boulder seat and grasped her shoulders.

"Do you feel the need of another friend?"

"That's beside the point."

"It's not. It's you I'm anxious about. I suppose I've never given you—well—something or other that Max is giving you right now—whatever it is. I'm not fool enough to think I could give you everything. . . . But I'm too blamed selfish to let another man give much of anything to you. I don't like poetry

—I couldn't in a thousand years. To me it simply tinkles, like a brook. I don't care for brooks. I like rush, action, a big stream dashing over the falls."

But now she surprised him. This time, at the declaration of his feeling about poetry, she did laugh.

It was low, irresistible laughter which shook her from head to foot. He watched her, his grim expression unrelaxed. She was quite enchanting in her laughter, but that didn't help her case much, to his mind. It was some time before she could speak, and then it was in response to his muttered:

"That's it, exactly. I suppose I'm very funny."

"Well—you almost are, dear. Poetry, to you, seems to be something that should be labeled 'poison'· and put high up on a shelf where nobody can get at it. Do you want poor Max to be more interested in the stock-market reports?"

"If I'd ever suspected he had poetry in him——"

It set her off again. And finally he smiled grudgingly.

"Of course I'm making an ass of myself. If you can laugh I suppose I can. We may as well go back. I don't want to kill the poor devil, even if he is in love with my wife. If I can just be sure—oh, God —*sure* . . ."

"You can be sure, Red."

He had to let it go at that. But he knew he wasn't going to be able to get the better of his infernal jealousy.

4

THE days went by. Max Buller grew slowly stronger. The talks and readings continued, always out under the trees not far from the cabin when the weather was right; inside by the fire when cool or wet days arrived. Everything was apparently in the open. Red came and went, did his best to be sporting about it, but his hazel eyes couldn't keep away from the two faces when he was near them. He couldn't know what was written on his own face and evident in his bearing. When he spoke to Max his tone was curt; he almost never joined the pair or sat with Max alone. And finally something happened.

He came back to the camp late one afternoon and found neither Ellen nor Max. He rushed about, looking for them. He questioned Brown.

"I don't know, Dr. Burns. Dr. Buller had me help him pack his bags. I sent down to the village for a car, and he went away in it. I haven't seen

Mrs. Burns at all since breakfast. She didn't say where she was going. Dr. Buller told me to give you this."

Brown produced a letter. Burns grasped at his own self-control. Of course there was an explanation. The two hadn't gone away together. That was unthinkable. And he mustn't give Brown, who was bound to be intensely curious, any cause to put two and two together and make five of them—which they couldn't make.

"Thanks, Brown. Mrs. Burns will be back soon, but Dr. Buller took us by surprise. We shall both be sorry to have him gone. We thought he meant to stay another week."

"Yes, sir. I'd thought for some time he was looking much better, but he seemed a little weaker when he went away than he has been, lately. I hope the journey won't be too much for him."

"Oh, no. He'll be all right."

Burns got away. He went out and strolled slowly down the trail, having lighted his pipe in view of Brown before he started. He had put the letter in his pocket, after having opened it and seemed to read it, though he hadn't read a word. He couldn't read it till he got out of sight.

He dreaded to read it. The handwriting, an odd characteristic scrawl, reminded him of Buller's notes on cases, sent to him at various times in past years. Short, meaningful phrases.

"I find the patient showing unmistakable symptoms of cardiac insufficiency. Mitral regurgitant murmur. Marked dilatation of the aorta. . . ."

This wasn't much like that, though it was a straightforward, briefly comprehensive statement of Dr. Maxwell Buller's own case, lacking scientific phrases.

DEAR RED:

I hardly know how to say to you what I must, and I take this way because I somehow can't tell you face to face. I am going away to Arizona for a while. These weeks here at the camp have been very wonderful to me—too wonderful for either your or my peace of mind. I am sure you know that I love Ellen. I couldn't help that, though I tried my best. I realize how generous you have been. I dare to think that Ellen cares for me too—but not in any way that could hurt you, Red.

I never had anybody in my life who meant much

to me until you came to practise in my town. I tried
to be a real friend to you—but you have been a
much greater one to me. If I go away now, without
any good-byes, it is because I am not quite strong
enough to say them—not even to Ellen. I have left
a note for her which she will show you—I want
her to.

Whether I shall ever come back I doubt. It doesn't
matter very much. You must not worry about that.
I have had my little glimpse of what I have missed
in life, and I am very grateful for that. It was only
a glimpse, Red—be sure of it. Of course you are
sure. You have her whole heart. She has only shown
me her friendship, but even so—I am a thousand
times richer than I ever expected to be.

God bless you both,

MAX.

Red sat staring at the irregular lines long after
he knew them by heart. Toward the close of the
note they had grown even more irregular; he could
guess easily enough what a task it had been to Max
to write them. He didn't know how he felt about
that note. At one moment relief, at the next com-

punction. It was his old, trusted friend who had written them, that was clear enough. Max Buller was exactly the honorable, loyal fellow Red had always known him to be. He had gone away because he couldn't endure any longer seeing what he couldn't have; it wasn't because he had had either hope or wish to take away from his friend Red what belonged to him. The more Red looked at that letter, in those straggling lines, the more pitiful he became. He hadn't been feeling pitiful toward Max for some time; now he was beginning to see what courage it must have taken for him to go away, and to put up all the barriers against his return by telling the whole story. Of course he couldn't and wouldn't come back. Red knew that . . . Some day there would be a newspaper notice—from Arizona. And that would be all.

5

BUT where was Ellen? He plunged on down the trail. She couldn't have gone far away from the camp; he knew her favorite places, one of them at least two miles from the cabin. If she had had a letter from Max to read, that would be where she had taken it. . . . A letter from Max. Red couldn't rest till he knew what was in it, and how Ellen had taken it, and how she was feeling now. Fear leaped up in him again. A letter. . . . Women treasured certain letters all their lives, he knew that. Many women had shown him letters. . . . One had shown him one of his own——brief, professional instructions as to what to do in his absence, with a word of friendly interest at the end. She had told him she should keep it always, and he had laughed and tried to joke her out of it. She had not been joked out of it. He had had to keep away from her. . . .

At some distance before the last bend in the trail beyond which was the spot where he hoped to find Ellen, she came slowly around a great boulder into sight. There was no letter in her hand. Where was it? Tucked into her dress——over her heart, perhaps? He knew women were like that. She was to show him that letter. Max himself had said so. Well, how was she looking? He could tell a lot by the first close view of her face.

But he must behave naturally, not like a jealous husband. This was no time for melodrama, of which he feared he had been guilty all too often in these last weeks. He went on to meet her.

"Hello! Thought you might be down this way. Been having a good rest all by yourself, dear?"

Her face was quiet, a little pale, perhaps, but— as he came near he saw that she had been weeping. Well—he must expect that. The whole thing had become pretty poignant. He himself, when he had read Max's letter, had felt a constriction in his throat. Gone off, all alone, to Arizona. . . . Red hated to think of that long journey on a hot train.

"Yes, all by myself. . . . I'm glad you came to meet me. I didn't realize how long I'd been gone."

"Tired?" He turned to walk with her, putting his arm about her. "Have anything to eat before you left?" He knew, from what Brown had said, that she hadn't.

"No. I didn't want it. . . . You know, of course, that Max has gone?"

"Brown told me. I'm sorry. But he left me a note that explained."

"Yes—he left me one."

There was a big loose bag on her arm, a vivid, striped thing, such as women use in the country. He hadn't noticed that, strangely enough. He had been looking for a letter in her hand. She put her hand in the bag and drew out the letter. She gave it to him. He took it with a strange reluctance, though up to that moment his whole thought had been upon it.

"Want me to read it?"

"Of course."

"Shall we wait till we get to the cabin? You're pretty tired."

"No, please read it now. Then——this can be over."

"Then let's sit down on this log. I'll read it, and then I'm going to take you home and put you to bed. You're all in."

She sat quietly while he read the note. After all, though it was longer, it said less than the one Max had left for Red.

DEAR ELLEN:

It seems like a queer return for all your kindness, my going off suddenly like this. But the time had come, I was sure, and I was selfish enough to leave you and Red in the way that would be easiest for me.

There are a great many things I'd like to say, but it's better not to try to say them. Only this:

Out where I'm going—it's a sanitarium for T. B., and a good one—there'll be other people I can be of some use to in a way I've never been capable of before. I'll be one with them. I've never been able to do much more than prescribe for my patients' physical symptoms; I've always been afraid to try to show them that I understood what was going on in their minds—which must always be a harder thing for them to bear than what goes on in their bodies. I couldn't talk with them about it. I've been shy and awkward, and though I've watched and envied Red a thousand times because he could give his patients and friends something that made all the difference with their recovery, I could never seem to learn for myself how to do it. Now I think I know —and you have taught me. As long as I live I shall be more grateful for that than for any of all the other kindnesses you and Red have shown me. Because as long as I live I shall want to be of use, and this is a way that has come only by my own illness. So I'm no longer minding much that I can't get well—as we have all known all along I couldn't.

I'd like to set down here the lines of Robert Browning that out of all you've read to me I now treasure most. Do you remember that you wrote them out for me? I'm taking that slip of paper away with me—it's all I'm taking.

The common problem, yours, mine, everyone's,
Is—not to fancy what were fair in life
Provided it could be,—but finding first
What may be, then find how to make it fair
Up to our means: a very different thing!

As always, your friend,
MAX.

Red folded the letter and slipped it into the envelope. He gave it back to Ellen, and she returned it to the bag on her arm. It was a long time before either spoke. Meanwhile Red had without attempt at concealment wiped away one hot tear after another. To himself he had been saying, over and over:

"*Old Max—old Max—old Max . . .*"

Then, finally: "Shall we go back, dear?"

They walked slowly along, Red's arm still about Ellen's shoulders. He knew her heart was very heavy, but his was so heavy too that he was sure they needed each other more than anything else in the world. When he should be able to say it he would tell her that she was to go on loving Max, as he would himself. Neither of them could want to help that, now. It was not every day that anyone got the chance to love one like Max.

LETTER from Dr. Burns to his sister, Anne Sutherland, in a sanitarium in Southern Italy.

DEAR ANNE:

I went to two funerals to-day. That's an odd way to start off a letter to an invalid, but according to your letter just received you're in pretty fair spirits because you know you're coming along properly. With your doctor promising you that you won't have any interference in locomotion when that leg and hip are mended, you've a right to be triumphant. Lucky you were to have clean breaks and no shattering of the bones. You don't know how lucky you were. So I can tell you about these things that are uppermost in my mind—I can't get away from them.

The funerals were of a rich man and a poor man. No, you're wrong. The rich man wasn't a hard, stingy, hated specimen of society, and the poor man wasn't a model of clean living and generosity to his poorer neighbors. They belonged to about the same stratum of society, and neither of them had had much money. One was a little old preacher who had also been a keen student all his life. At ninety-four he was still eagerly doing research work by means of a paid reader's eyes and his own brains, and writing articles giving his conclusions on matters pertaining to theology, philosophy, science. Not three days before he died he told me that while he knew he wasn't going to have time to work much longer in that book-walled study of his, he had no doubt whatever that he'd be allowed to go on with his studies in some celestial workshop, with unlimited sources of knowledge at his disposal. His face, as he said it, showed how rich he felt himself to be. When we laid him away he still had that look— he'd always had it since I'd known him—of being ready for the next thing he could learn. If all great scholars could be as certain as he that the limits of their chance to explore weren't those of this life, what a lot more zest they could put into their labors. That's what my old man called it: "I'm just getting ready to be taught, Dr. Burns," he said. Who can say he wasn't right?

The other man—whom I'm calling desperately poor—was only thirty-six when he turned on the gas and put himself out. He had a comfortable home, a wife and children, but he never, so far as I could

*see, had been pleased or satisfied with anything.
Everything was wrong with everybody, from his
point of view. He was the gloomiest fellow I ever
knew, and the grouchiest. Of course, this attitude of
mind was at least partially a disease—an inheritance
—the wires crossed somewhere—a short circuit
burning out the machinery. Yet I vow no psycho-
analyst could have wholly explained him. He had a
fair intelligence, could see that he was on the wrong
track, half wanted to get on the right one, but
wouldn't set the switch to put himself there. "What
the hell——" was his favorite phrase. And I declare
to you that when I saw him gone I felt like con-
gratulating his family. There's no question whatever
in my mind that we can set our own switches, Anne.
My little old preacher had set his, with all the force
of his feeble body and strong will, to keep himself
on the track long after life would have shunted him
onto a siding. And it was owing to his faith that
life was worth living because it was, as he said, only
a preparation, to be made the most of, for the Big
Chance coming in the next world. And even if he
was wrong—dead wrong—which I don't believe—
wasn't he a rich man all his days?*

Well, what a preachment! You'll be glad I don't

go to funerals every day. Somehow these two cases, in apposition, got hold of my imagination. And of course you must know that I am missing my little old preacher to-night. No talk with him but made me richer myself. I had to write of him, if of anything. After all, I can't be cutting up capers to amuse you in every letter, though that's what you probably expect of me. Next time, perhaps. My best love, anyhow.

RED.

VI

WHEN Mr. George Graham and his daughter Eleanora left the Graham camp, after their week-end visit with Dr. and Mrs. Burns, to whom they had lent it, the Great Airplane Contest was not yet settled. Red, appealed to by the aroused and worried father, had done his best to be judicial and fair to both.

"It's just a question, I should say," he pointed out, "as to what qualities you most want to bring out in your daughter. Since she's not financially independent of you, you can prevent her from doing what you disapprove of—to a certain extent. Undoubtedly she could find some means to carry out her will, which seems to be very strong."

"It's always been strong. That's why she's made so many mistakes. But this one—why, this is worse than marrying the wrong man twice. This—why, she might easily lose her life, Dr. Burns."

"Yes. I might lose mine to-morrow, in the same way. Yet thousands of miles are flown in safety every day, and thousands will be flown in greater safety to-morrow. You couldn't buy my plane from me at any price if I couldn't get another the next day. And as between the motor road and the skies, I'm beginning to think there's not much choice. Look at this morning's headlines. The front page is literally covered with the accounts of smashes, the hospitals are full of the mangled. Yet we don't run our cars into the garages and nail up the doors."

"No—of course not."

"I know of a rich mother who spent any amount of her money to keep her young son from flying. She bought him a yacht; she sent him abroad to buy the most expensive foreign car on the market. And then he ran his car into a tree, in Italy—and that ended it. She couldn't keep him safe by pitting her will against his."

"No," admitted Graham. "We don't know the safe places in life. At the same time . . ."

The Grahams had gone away without having settled the question. Red, however, hadn't much doubt of the outcome. He himself thought Eleanora would make a successful flier. Bob, much interested, had tried her out with various impromptu devices for testing her equilibrium and nerve control. He whirled her about, made her walk a chalk line blindfold; made experiments with her eyesight, her hearing, her power to react instantaneously to a suggestion. He all but stood her on her head. They had had a great time of it, and Bob had predicted that when she should go into a training school and should be put to such real tests as they could give her there, she would find no hindrance to the starting of her instruction. Meanwhile, at Eleanora's insistence, Dr. Burns had examined her heart and made some other tests. He had assured her that she was probably physically sound, though she should be looked over more carefully at some clinic.

"Of course, you've been too lazy," he said bluntly. "You haven't done half enough exercise. You've probably danced enough, and dancing's good as far as it goes. But you should be playing tennis, swimming, riding——"

"I've done all those things," protested Eleanora.

"Pretty moderately. You should now do 'em for your life. Spend the rest of the summer getting yourself in trim; then see what they say to you at a flying school. Pick out the best. That is—if you settle it with your father."

"Haven't I a right to do what I want to, whether Father agrees or not?"

"Hurt him as little as you can," advised Burns. "Persuade him, don't try to knock him down. Eventually he'll be proud of you, if I know a determined young woman when I see one."

2

IT WAS three months before he heard from Eleanora. She was in a Southern flying school, and her father was staying temporarily at a great hotel near by.

"He's unhappy," she wrote. "But I'm wild about it all. I'm going to make a pilot, so my instructor says. And Father is getting a fine coat of tan to take North with him. I really think he's weakening in his opposition. To tell the truth, I think he *almost* thinks the sight of me, full of life and enthusiasm as I am, is worth his worry. Anyhow, it's a different kind of worry from that he's had over me ever since I made my first crazy marriage, at seventeen. I'm enclosing a snapshot of me, that you may see what a difference clothes do make! I shall never forget my first trip, with you, arrayed in flimsy evening things. And how absurd I felt beside Betty Bevan!"

It didn't seem quite possible that the subject of

that photograph could be Miss Eleanora Graham. The flying suit, the carelessly natural attitude beside the plane, the sun on her face, the light in her eyes, the bright gravity of her lips. . . .

"That's not the same girl, Dad," said Bob, gazing over his father's shoulder at the picture. "She's all made over already. It's not that she couldn't be a clothes model any more, or give a fellow an eyeful and an earful while she danced with him. I'd hate to have her lose all that—er—whatever it is she pulls. But—I like her better this way. And I'd like to hear her talk. Too bad she's 'way down South where we can't check up on her evolution."

"Considering the brand of weather up here"—it was late November now, and the Burnses had long since left the Graham camp and returned to their home—"it's a good thing she's where she is. A good thing for other reasons."

3

GEORGE GRAHAM, returning North with the spring, came by Burns's office and made his own report.

"I feel better about her in one way, Doctor. You were right in insisting that she needed a complete change in interests. She seems to have found that. I never saw her so vigorous. But—I seem only to have changed the form of my anxieties. I think of her night and day, not knowing when something will happen."

"I understand, Mr. Graham. But you never knew what would happen before. Nobody knows. Now, I'm flying right along, and not hesitating to take my wife with me, often. We have the best of planes, the surest of pilots, and I myself have become not the poorest of fliers, though I never take over the controls when I have Ellen or Bob along. Of course, I don't know when something may go wrong. But— I can imagine a worse fate than my wife and I dropping out of life together. It would be a gorgeous way to go."

"Ah, but suppose one of you went and the other stayed? That's what I have to face."

"Haven't you been up with your daughter?" questioned Red with a searching look.

"No. . . . I can't seem to overcome my— reluctance."

"She's a licensed pilot by now?"

"Yes. She's had what they call so many 'flying hours' alone. I have forgotten how many. They call her one of the most promising of the newcomers."

"Is she back in the North?"

"Yes. Not a hundred miles from our home." He named the airport. "She's taken a small apartment with a friend, not far from there."

"Go up with her some day, in perfect flying weather," advised Red.

"Well, I——"

"Don't tell me," blurted Red, "that you love her and yet aren't willing to risk your life—since you feel you'd be doing that—just once with her."

Graham stiffened. His lips moved, but he made no reply. His color changed a little.

"That was a mean shot," Red acknowledged quickly. "I'm sorry. . . . See here. Try it out with me. I'll let my pilot fly us, though I admit I'm jealous the minute I give things into his hands. It's a good day to-day. I won't keep you up over half an hour, or go up over a couple of thousand feet. We'll fly on an even keel—no scares."

But Graham wouldn't go. Burns was sure he understood. There was a horror to the older man in places that were high. He was afraid he wouldn't acquit himself with courage. And it partially accounted for his more than ordinary fears for his daughter—for whom he needn't have feared excessively, because of that cool nerve which is the first asset of the flier. Eleanora had it—she had had it when she had made those two marriages; had had it when she had flown with Burns himself, in the night, beside a form which might even at that moment have been growing rigid. . . .

4

ONE day there was a picture in the Sunday editions of Eleanora, taken at a great flying meet. She was standing with Betty Bevan, who had broken another record, and a crowd was all about. Eleanora wasn't facing the camera, but her face was sufficiently revealed to show her pleasure in the other's accomplishment. Her name was given. Probably not because she as yet amounted to anything as a flier, but because her father's name was one well known, and she was a friend of Miss Bevan. No cameraman could have resisted taking her, anyhow, Red and Bob and Ellen agreed.

Now and then brief letters came from Eleanora, or cards, from one place or another. She was getting on with her flying, she hoped before long to be able to qualify for one of the shorter air races or endurance tests always taking place somewhere. She was perfectly content. She had had two or three narrow escapes from serious accidents, but she was lucky and had come out of them with nothing worse than a cracked wing or a forced landing in a spot not intended for landing. Please don't let her father know about these little incidents, she begged. They happened to everybody. In fact, if they didn't happen to you you didn't learn. She had thus far succeeded in keeping any notice of such mishaps out of the papers which he was accustomed to read.

"Some day she'll get one, though," prophesied Bob. "She's the sort that'll take chances. She's got Betty Bevan ahead of her, and she wants to be at least Betty's runner up. She can't make it, but she'll try."

5

ONE early morning there came a long-distance call. The voice at the other end, when Burns finally got it, was hardly recognizable in spite of evident effort to make it strong and quiet.

"Dr. Burns—this is George Graham. Graham— yes. Eleanora's father. . . . My daughter has had an accident. . . . They tell me not to be alarmed—but I am. . . . It happened yesterday, but they couldn't locate me—the fools in my office—till this minute. It's two hundred miles—Boston. . . . She's in a hospital. . . . Dr. Burns, I want you to see her—I must have you see her. . . . Will you take me—in your airplane?"

Would Burns take him? Red was astonished—yet not astonished—at the request. In his most reassuring tones he made the arrangements. He would pick Mr. Graham up at an airport near the city from which he had called, not more than thirty miles away. He would be there in no time at all, he had only to be rushed out in his car to the field where he now kept his plane.

Seldom had Red responded to a call which stirred him more. If anything had happened really to injure Eleanora permanently . . . He didn't want to think of that. Strange that Graham, who must feel that it was Burns himself who was responsible for Eleanora's taking to adventuring in the clouds, should want him to carry her father to her. Doubtless Graham's conviction that he owed his own life to the red-headed surgeon was influencing him. That, and the notion that he would rather go with

a friend than with a stranger, if he was to fly. Fly!
—George Graham himself had asked to be flown!
He had forgotten his fears; no, his anxiety had over-
ridden them, of course, as any father's would. Nothing strange in that. Well—it wouldn't be as easy
a flight as it might be. It wasn't perfect flying
weather this morning. Clouds hung low, it was raining and a little foggy. It was early September, but
the air felt like April, chill and raw. No matter.
Burns would have flown "blind" to get George
Graham to his daughter.

Red and his pilot, landing, found Mr. Graham
waiting, pallid of face but apparently keeping a
grip upon himself.

"I tried to telephone the hospital from here," he
said, "but they haven't got the call through, and I
don't want to wait, since you're here."

"We'll make the distance before they get the call
through," Red said cheerfully, "if it's like some that
get hung up. Up you go, Mr. Graham—step there
—and there. I can't tell you how glad I am to be
taking you myself."

"I had to have you," Graham answered, in a low
voice, hardly to be heard above the humming of the
plane, as it waited to be off.

It was the last word he said for two hundred miles. The trip was a hard one for him, no doubt of that. It would have been for any novice. Even the experienced pilot had to resort to this and that device for overcoming the low visibility which accompanied them at least half of the distance. When rising winds finally blew the fog away they brought fresh conditions of discomfort. For a few moments they ran through a rather violent squall. There was no "even keel" on which to depend. Red had to minister to his passenger more than once when the unavoidable rough riding of the plane laid him low. Yet Graham behaved admirably, he thought. The man was game, after all; he made no signs of distress beyond those nobody could have helped, under the conditions.

It was over at last. The landing at the airport which marked the end of the journey was made in brilliant sunshine though in a high wind. A motor was waiting—Graham had wired ahead for that. The pair got into it, and Graham's pallor lessened slightly as they were whirled away.

"A fairly quick trip, in spite of all the bad weather," Red observed. "You wouldn't have been more than well started by this time, by train."

"No," assented Graham. "No. I'm thankful to be here."

At the great city hospital, though it was one which had never heard of either of the two men who presently besieged it, red tape was cut with amazing rapidity by Dr. Burns, who had never yet been halted by a barrier stretched across his course. There was something about him which marked him for one whom small officials didn't refuse.

So in less than ten minutes—a brief period enough, as those who have sat in hospital waiting rooms well know—they had the report that Miss Graham was not seriously injured, the extent being a broken arm and a bruised shoulder and hip; that she had recovered from all shock; that Mr. Graham and Dr. Burns might be brought up at once.

Graham wiped his brows, smiling faintly.

"But I shall not be satisfied till you have looked her over," he said. "They might have missed something."

"It's splendid," replied Burns with a friendly grin, "to have anybody feel like that about one. But I don't think they're likely to overlook things in this place. The first glance will reassure you, I've no doubt."

A pleasantly starchy nurse ushered them into the large private room. Burns, looking over the top of Graham's head, saw for himself. Well! Could this be Eleanora? Impossible!

"Hello, Dad!" said a gay voice. "Expected to find me in a dozen pieces, did you? Nothing of the kind. I had amazing luck!"

Her father went up to her and bent down. For a moment he seemed incapable of speech. Burns, deferring his own greeting, turned aside to the nurse.

"Easy to tell by that voice she's doing as well as she was reported to be," he said, in a low tone.

"Oh, yes," agreed the smiling nurse. "She really had a wonderful escape. The ambulance men who brought her in said she could have landed safely if she hadn't done something to avoid hitting somebody that ran out across the field. I don't understand it, of course, but I guess that's true. I asked her about it, and she couldn't deny it. But she didn't describe it to me."

"Well!" said Burns again to himself. He could hardly wait till Graham finally turned about and summoned him. Graham's face was beaming. Red came up to the bed. An enormous mass of red roses was beside it, lending color to the whole room.

Eleanora was so tanned that her fair hair seemed fairer than ever. Her eyes were deeply happy; one might almost have said that she looked radiant. She stretched up a brown arm from which the white linen of the hospital garment she wore was rolled to the shoulder. Even the ugliness of this standardized attire couldn't dim her brightness. As Burns grasped her hand he felt the firmness of it; it was a hand which had learned to do something important. As for her smile, it was nothing short of dazzling.

"You two," she said, "dashing across country in a plane to see my little injuries! What fun to have you both. Really worth it, to know my father has 'taken off,' at last. He'll never mind it again. I'll have him up with me, now. But it took you to get him up."

"It did nothing of the sort," countered Burns. "He ordered me, he ordered the plane, he ordered the speed of the flight, he ordered everything. He functioned as a chief executive, if ever anybody did. I should have said he was at least the president of an airways corporation."

George Graham was smiling now, himself. He took a chair beside the bed. The nurse brought up another for Burns, on the other side. The latter made a slight gesture which the nurse recognized. Of course he was a doctor—nobody else would have done it with just that slight tip-back of the head toward the door accompanied by a friendly look at her which said as plainly as words: "Just step outside for a few minutes, eh?" She went out, unoffended, though she would certainly have liked to stay. That red head, those hazel eyes under their dark brows, that whole arresting presence; she wished he belonged in this hospital. There were some interesting men on the staff, but nobody—no, nobody like this one. No wonder Miss Graham had wanted him brought up with her father. "Oh, yes, *yes!*" Miss Graham had said. Who wouldn't? thought the nurse, and envied her patient more than ever.

"It wasn't much of an executive," denied Eleanora's father. "Except in the matter of speed. I believe I did say we couldn't go too fast for me."

"We could have gone much faster if it hadn't been for fog," explained Burns. "No use taking chances on your father's first flight. By the way, I understand you crashed your plane to avoid hitting some fool who ran across your path?"

"Now, where," questioned Eleanora, "did you get that?"

"Nurse. True, isn't it?"

"I was making a bad landing. I only made it a little badder on his account."

Burns nodded. "You score," he said. "You belong. That's the answer that marks the clan. How badly did you crack up the ship?"

"Hardly at all. One wing—the tip. And one propeller blade—just a bit. We really nosed over quite gently. And me—why, look how I came out. I could be up and off again this minute if it wasn't for this left arm—*left*. Wasn't that luck?"

"Luck it was. And a trifle of nerve. Simple diagnosis." Burns was smiling broadly now. He would have liked to give Eleanora a good hug, just out of pride in her valor—avoiding that left arm, of course. He would have done it, except for Mr. George Graham. Mr. Graham, he had an idea, wouldn't wholly understand these semi-professional amenities.

The nurse opened the door and came softly back.

"Please excuse me, Miss Graham," she said, and brought a calling card over to the bedside. Eleanora took it, glanced at it, glanced at the red roses, glowing like a fire beside the head of her bed. Then she showed the card to her father. A strange look came into his face—almost an eager look. His eyes met his daughter's.

"Do you wish to see him?" he asked.

"I—yes, I believe I do," she answered.

"Shall we go? Till he has gone?"

"I think I'd rather you stayed—both of you—if you will."

Burns, who had risen, sat down again.

The nurse went out. It must be hard on nurses, doing all the routine work over their patients, and then having to be out of things just when they become interesting.

6

ELEANORA held out the card to Burns, who read "Mr. Courtney Brace" upon it—which meant nothing at all to him. Probably one of Eleanora's fellow fliers. The news of the accident was undoubtedly in the afternoon papers, by now.

"It's my husband," she said. "That is—he was my husband, two years ago. He wasn't flying then. He is now. But we haven't met."

"I really think I'd better go," Burns urged, though naturally he was now more than ever wishing to stay.

Eleanora shook her head. Her word had to be law. Burns felt an enormous curiosity about Eleanora's former husband, who had sent an armful of red roses ahead of him on the first call he was paying her since they bade each other good-bye. Why was he coming now? Had he too seen her photograph in the papers and wanted to discover for himself how she had changed since they had presumably tired of each other? He must have changed, himself. Flying did seem to change people, particularly those who had been more or less bored with themselves or with other people before. Interest in life certainly did seem to pick up with these new and thrilling experiences.

The door opened again. A black-haired, dark-eyed, and deeply bronzed young man wearing flying clothes came in. Everything seemed to be black about him, except, presently, for a slight gleam of very white teeth when he opened his lips. He stood looking across at Eleanora.

Mr. Graham got up and advanced in a dignified manner, extending his hand.

"How do you do, Courtney," he said.

The young man met him halfway, grasping his hand, unsmiling.

"How do you do, Mr. Graham."

"Mr. Brace, Dr. Burns," said Mr. Graham.

The two shook hands.

"These confounded preliminaries," thought Burns, and now he did wish himself out of the room. What about the meeting between the once married pair? How could they meet with anything like naturalness with two witnesses present? Of course they couldn't.

"How do you do, Court," said Eleanora. She stretched out that tanned arm, and he came toward her. "Mighty nice of you to send the roses."

"How do you do, Lee?" he said, and bent over and took the hand. This time the salutation was a question. "As well as you look?"

"Even better than I look. There's really nothing the matter to speak of."

"I just read about it an hour ago," he said.

"Won't you sit down?"

"May I?" He drew up a chair.

"I saw your picture in the papers a month ago," he said. "Beside your ship."

"Did you? I saw yours—six months ago—beside *your* ship."

Burns broke parole. Something in Eleanora's face

told him, used to reading signs in faces, that she now regretted having insisted upon witnesses to this meeting. The young man looked to Burns like a particularly nice fellow, virile and attractive—and immensely interested in his former wife. It was certainly no place for spectators. Red rose and quietly walked out of the room. Nobody bade him remain.

A moment after his exit Mr. Graham joined him in the hall. Nobody, evidently, had insisted upon his remaining, either.

To Burns's surprise, Mr. Graham looked almost happy.

7

THEY walked down the noiseless tiled floor of the long corridor together without speaking, toward a window seemingly a mile away. When they reached it they sat down on the window sill. Nobody was in sight except an orderly in the far distance, wheeling an empty stretcher.

"I'm going to say to you, since you've seen so much," said Mr. Graham, speaking in the near whisper which is usage in hospital corridors, "I should be glad—thankful—to have this result in a re-marriage. I always liked Courtney. It wasn't he who seemed tired of Eleanora: it was she who became restless. He is a number of years older than she, and somewhat more staid. But now——"

"Now," said Burns, "he doesn't look too staid for any girl. I suppose it's those flying clothes—they give a look of adventure to any man. I like his face."

"Yes, I like his face—I like him. I couldn't see why . . . but just now she looked as though she were glad to see him. Didn't you think so?"

"Very much. And if he sent her those roses—as I suspect he did, and she knew he was coming, and she had that—well—that decidedly lighted-up look on her face because she was expecting him, why, I'd be willing to gamble a considerable sum on . . . You see, they'd have a common interest, now. They'd be flying together."

"Yes, flying together," mused George Graham. "Flying together." He turned and gazed down out of the window for a minute, at an absolutely blank courtyard, but as though he saw there something that gave him comfort.

"You know, Dr. Burns," he said, turning back, "it would be a great deal to me to feel that Eleanora had a husband with her. She's going to keep on flying, and I—have to keep on thinking about her flying. If she could have——"

He paused so long that Burns finished it for him: "A flying partner? Yes, I can see what a satisfaction that would be to you. I don't wonder."

There was another long pause. Something in his companion's thin ageing face kept Burns from taking the lead and talking on. He felt that there was something more coming, and that it was important. It came, at last, the thing that, once having heard, he wished he might have heard long ago.

"Dr. Burns, my only son Gordon, Eleanora's brother, was in the Great War. He went over early, and he flew too, with a British squadron that saw combat. He was—shot down over the enemy lines. He was buried over there. . . . Perhaps you can see that . . . can see why I——"

Burns saw it all. Graham didn't need to tell him another word. In his own heart was an immense respect.

LETTER from Dr. Burns to his sister, Mrs. Richard Sutherland, in London, where she has rejoined her husband.

DEAR ANNE:

Yes, I'm afraid I've rather let down on writing you, since I knew you were up and about again, the hip and leg functioning as properly as could be expected, and your report of your weight down to— well, as near what it ought to be as any young woman of your deep-rooted affection for sweets could be asked to bring it. If I've irritatingly borne on that, Anne, it's because a medical man and brother has understood that only a constant dropping of advice could wear away the stone. (About ten stone, using the British unit of weight, would be just about right for your height, and I consider myself remarkably clever to have made that nice little play on the word, eh?)

Ellen and I are mighty glad to know that you and Dick are together again, and that the rascal looked good to you when you saw his face. I had an idea he would, my dear. And I know precisely how you *looked to him, after he'd had his fill of being free to bounce around without you, which I have no doubt he badly needed. A lucky accident it was that floored you, after all—now, wasn't it? It's odd how a personality you think you're so intimately familiar with that there can be nothing new about it takes on freshness when you've been separated from it for a while. Sometimes for better, sometimes for worse—and it's for better, in your and Dick's case, I know, for you're both far from being stereotyped and commonplace. You know, Anne, I have a notion that after several months of your handsome Italian doctor's and other attachés paying you artificial compliments, Dick's good old American bluntness wasn't so unacceptable after all.*

So you're coming home. To the plushy apartment, Anne? That same apartment, fourteen stories up; the same doorman (I detest that doorman, his nose turns up so oddly), the same general round of everything you had before? The same friends, the same parties, the same boredom—don't tell me you didn't have a lot of that—the same (I'm going to speak even more plainly than usual) lack of a job? For it's my opinion that you and Dick both need a job more than you need anything in the world. If you don't look out, for lack of that job, you're going to be bored all over again.

I'm not such a fool as not to appreciate that rich and full lives can be lived—are constantly lived—inside those great structures of steel and stone. It all depends on the people who live there, and what they bring to the living. Splendid jobs are done inside some of them—real homes exist—children grow up in them, and they are not starved for want of the vital ingredients in the mental and spiritual food fed to them. But—it's never seemed to me—well, Anne, to be as brutally honest as I must be—that you and Dick got enough fresh air in that apartment of yours—it's always seemed to me pretty stuffy—and you know I don't mean literal lack of oxygen. I think it's the people who surround you that vitiate that air. They would, for me: I'd gasp and die in it.

Of course, I can't prescribe the kind of roof I'd like to see you under, making a try at a new sort of thing. But I can tell you what I think might be there with you, under any roof, making it a place to stay. You need something to do, every blessed day, that nobody else could do quite so well as you. I'm about to offer you a real job—the realest one there is. To save your soul as well as your body from the flesh-

pots, Anne. In the end, the fleshpots always become empty, take my word for it. And then what?

Listen, Anne.

I've been keeping an eye for three months on a baby girl who is turning out one of the prettiest babies I've ever seen in my life—for one of that age. She should be pretty—her mother and father had all the good looks in the world. Yes, she's illegitimate. I detest the word. As if any little human body God has breathed life into could be anything but legitimately a member of society, with all its rights and privileges. The two young people weren't married, and wouldn't marry, for reasons I won't go into here. Both were of good blood. And both died within a month of the child's birth, under the strangest possible conditions. The whole affair was known to none of the relatives, who would have had nothing to do with the child if they had known. The nurse and I were the only two who understood the situation. The nurse can be trusted absolutely. I've known her for years.

The child is in a crêche, waiting for adoption. She would have been adopted a hundred times over before now—there's always a long waiting list for such babies. But I've managed to keep a hand on her—for you. Not until you say you don't want her shall I take my hand off, and even then Ellen and I shall be mightily tempted to bring her home with us. The mite would attract a heart of stone, Anne—and your heart and Dick's are made of something softer than that, even though you've deliberately hardened them against children since you lost the two that never lived, in the early days of your marriage. I've never believed you couldn't successfully have had others, in spite of the famous professional opinions you've had (and paid heavily for) on the subject. But let that go—you think you can't, and I understand why.

But this baby—well—— Ah, come on, Anne! It would make all the difference. Think it over. Dick too. I'll bet he'll be the first to give in when he sees those deep blue eyes.

Life ought to grow richer instead of poorer, as it goes on. I can swear it does. It's tremendously interesting, at every stage, if one takes it as it comes and makes the most of it. I've packed mine pretty full, thus far. And I intend to go on packing it full, even though the time comes by and by when I can't tear about as I do now. I can always care what happens around me. I can keep myself from becoming dull to it. The Lord take me before that happens! I'd rather be stabbed in the back by an unseen enemy and put out of it altogether than turn a stolid, sullen face on life.

When I see you, as I hope to soon now, I shall have a world of things to tell you that couldn't be put into letters. Plenty of things have happened, human drama has been staged, in which Ellen and I have taken part. Until you come, then, Sis—and mind you don't put on another ounce of weight on the way home!

Always,
RED.

VII

"NEARLY ready, Red?"

"As nearly ready as I ever shall be for one of these big dinners. This is *one* time when I'd welcome the voice of that telephone, but of course it'll be silent to-night. I won't make a speech in that place —I won't, you know, Ellen."

"You won't? Not even when they begin: 'We have with us to-night our most distinguished——'"

"Hi, let me look at you! I hadn't caught sight of you since I was dazzled by that slick shiny white thing you wear under everything. Those outlines of yours, Len—well—but they aren't lost even under all that fluff of black. Let me kiss your beautiful bare arm right here . . . and this shoulder . . . and next—thank heaven you never use stuff on your lips—don't need to——"

"Dearest, you really mustn't become infatuated with me right now, when we're all but late. Remember how upset Colonel Dowling is when everybody isn't on time for one of his dinners. Here's your collar."

The branch telephone by Red's bed rang. Red's face, temporarily illumined by his survey of his wife looking her loveliest in evening array, had gloomed over again at the presentation to him of the collar of his dress shirt. But it promptly now became cheerful once more—even hopeful. Well did Ellen know that he would welcome almost any summons to a bedside rather than go to a formal dinner and be called upon—without more than two minutes' warning—for an impromptu speech.

"Yes," said Red, with eagerness, into the transmitter. "Yes, of course. I'll drive over right away."

" 'Yes, of course!' " she said, imitating successfully his own warmly assenting tone. "I knew it would come. It's all right, dear. . . . Are you perfectly sure you didn't engage Bob to call you up from somewhere?"

"Not this time. It was Bob Black, not our Bobby."

"Oh! I hope none of them are ill, over there."

"He didn't say, so I imagine not. He didn't say anything, except to ask me to come over. He added: 'I need you, Red.' That's all the summons I have to have from him. He doesn't call me up for nothing."

Ellen agreed. It was an old friendship, dating from the days of the Great War, when Robert Black had left a worshipful parish to be the sort of fighting chaplain who went over the top with his men, while Red, chafing under Dr. Max Buller's explanation that he couldn't get by the army examinations because of an unsound heart, had stayed behind and watched the newspaper columns. When the young Scotsman, Black, had first come to the prominent church which Red had attended now and then to please Ellen—and from which ushers with messages had usually extracted him by the time he was well seated—Red had been in a state of extreme prejudice against the clergy in general, and considered most of them mushrooms, not men. But he had gradually been won to the ardent support of this member of the profession by Black's ability, virility, and personal winsomeness of a most sturdy sort. Burns had ultimately become convinced by Black that he could no more condemn a whole profession because of occasional failures to come up to standards of honesty and loyalty than he could dismiss all the practitioners of medicine and surgery because a small proportion of them belonged in the ranks of the charlatans.

Though Black was no longer in Red's suburban town, but was minister of a great church in the large city, twelve miles away, the two met as often as they could manage it. Black had married Jane Ray, who had once been in the ranks of the charming young scoffers at religion, but who had learned in the time of her war service that Robert Black's beliefs were not after all too difficult to accept, and that they really meant something tangible and workable in a world of doubt. To the Burnses the marriage of these two was a particularly happy one, and the four were closely bound together in interests and affection.

Red now slid out of his despised evening clothes and into his daytime tweeds with the celerity of one used to responding to hurry calls. He kissed his wife again, in a decidedly more detached fashion than before, expressing his regret that she must depend upon friends to take her to Colonel Dowling's dinner—"Too bad, Len, but the Chesters'll be delighted"—and ran down the stairs. Two minutes later he backed his powerful, low-hung roadster out of his garage—the car he preferred when he wasn't bothering with a chauffeur—and was off.

In no time at all he drew up before the gray stone manse which stood in the shadow of the stately church in the crowded city, noting that there were few lights in the windows, and none upstairs, a sure sign that nobody was ill. Black's study windows alone were bright, but the shades were drawn. Red strode up the hedge-bordered walk to the low door-stone, tried the door, and finding it unlocked made his way in and straight to that study. Saturday evening seldom found Black anywhere else.

The door opened instantly at his knock, and his friend stood before him: a tall, well built figure, straight shouldered, with a face such as men trust. The whole look of him challenged one's attention.

"Here I am," said Red, questions in his eyes.

"Here you are," said Black, "on the very heels of your promise. It was great of you to come—I knew you would. I hope I didn't take you away from anything important. I'm afraid I didn't stop to inquire about that."

"Nothing less important could have been on my schedule. One of that codfish Dowling's robustious dinners. I never was more glad to hear my phone ring."

"I'd put off calling you as long as I could, but

to-night my wish to talk with you became a pressing need. I couldn't seem to get ready to preach to-morrow without you to see me through."

"What's up? When you need anybody to see you through anything there's something vitally wrong. Come—out with it. Don't waste time, man."

Black knew his friend Red. Not more than sixty seconds had been wasted since the door opened and closed, but even those were too many for a red-headed consultant in an emergency.

"Sit down—even if I don't. I seem to want to walk."

"Walk, then—and talk. I've been worried to death all the way out here."

"It's not so easy to begin, Red. A queer thing has happened. I can't find Jane—since yesterday morning. And this is Saturday night."

"Can't find Jane! You mean—she's disappeared? *Jane?*"

Black nodded, his brow contracting.

"Go ahead. Pour it out. Don't make me question you, lad."

"I won't. We had breakfast together yesterday morning. I had to speak at a convention and didn't get home for lunch. I came in at four, and she wasn't here. Mrs. Hodder hadn't seen her, nor Della, the maid, since breakfast. She'd left no word. You know how many engagements she has, but you know how orderly she is about them. She never leaves me guessing where she is. I've kept fairly cool, being sure there was some explanation—a note for me I'd missed, or a message from wherever she was that somebody'd failed to deliver. So far I haven't done much inquiring—didn't want to stir up things and set tongues wagging—they do wag about any minister's household, always. With every hour I've been absolutely confident I'd have some word. Jane's so competent to take care of herself, you know."

"Yes, I know."

Red didn't put into words his professional re-action to this news. Amnesia—loss of memory—it did hit people, anywhere. Yet Jane didn't seem in the least the sort of young woman to have that happen to her. His glance went to the large framed photograph of her which stood always upon the polished surface of the massive desk near the front windows of the big study. It was that of a beautiful, distinguished-looking woman of not more than thirty-five years, her features youthfully mature, her whole appearance suggesting a sort of delicate

strength to be relied upon—as Red well knew it
could be. Mrs. Robert McPherson Black was not
only the wife of the most prominent minister in the
city; she, as well as he, belonged among the socially
elect, quite without effort on the part of either to
hold that position. Apparently nothing of im-
portance in public affairs could be done without the
presence of the pair, yet they seemed much more
absorbed in the fortunes of the poor and the young
of both parish and city than in making themselves
sought after by the rich and prosperous anywhere.
No, it was inconceivable that Jane, in perfect health
as she was, walking rapidly along a street, whether
in this or any other town, could have suddenly lost
her memory.

"But this—is Saturday evening," Black went on
hurriedly. "You know our ways. No matter how
busy we are through the week, we keep Saturday
evening clear, unless impossible. Jane is always at
home with me for dinner at seven—we ask nobody
in—she spends the evening with me in this room.
Together we get ready—for Sunday."

Red knew this. It came of being a Scotsman, born
of generations of Sabbath-keeping habits which
began the evening before. Modern enough though

Robert Black was, he still thought about this special preparedness for the great day coming. Undoubtedly in that preparedness lay one of the secrets of his unusual power.

"And when she didn't come to-night you really got anxious—of course."

"Disturbed, at least, in spite of all the explanations I can think of. I can't conceive of her letting Saturday evening pass, no matter where she was, without calling me up or wiring me. Yet I won't say I'm anxious—except to hear."

"But you can't—" said Red, getting up from sitting on the arm of the big chair Black had indicated, which was the nearest Red had come to making himself comfortable as an ordinary caller might—comfortable, with his friend in this trouble —"you can't go on waiting for her to come without taking any steps to find her. You'll have to begin to throw out some kind of a line to pull her in."

"She always carries," said Black, "in her purse or somewhere about her, a card with her name and address. So do I. I suppose it was a follow-up of the identification tags we both wore for a year and a half over there. It seems only a reasonable precaution. So—if anything had happened———"

They went over it, discussing probabilities. Red was all for letting the authorities know, insisting that there was no use in taking chances on something having happened after which there would have been no means taken to inform anybody. Black was all against it—as yet. He was stubborn about it, as Scotch as Scotch, said Red to himself. Not before Monday, at the earliest, Black declared.

"I suppose you've telephoned Cary," said Red suddenly. He too was now pacing the floor. The two men met and passed on their way to the ends of the long room with the regularity of a clock.

Cary Ray was Jane's brother. He had been a war correspondent, and afterward had married a girl named Fanny Fitch, who had been a gay young entertainer in leave areas, and had sometimes made her way well up toward the front. Black and Red together had made Cary fit to go by seeing him through months of recovery from a nervous break-down caused by wild drinking and other excesses. The war experience had seemed to make two decidedly irresponsible and reckless young people over into sane beings. Red now recalled that he hadn't heard much about them, down in New York, for considerable time. But he knew that no matter how Cary might change, he and his sister Jane would never cease to care deeply for each other.

"I couldn't telephone him," explained Black. "He and Fanny have been abroad for months. Didn't we tell you that? They gave up their apartment—they never furnished one for themselves—always rushing about—that's their natures. They haven't let us know anything about themselves for a long time —Jane's been unhappy about it—feared Cary'd gone to drinking heavily again."

"You're actually going to wait till Monday, Bob, before you do anything definite?"

Black paused in his walk. "I am doing something definite," he said, "with every breath I draw. But I'm giving Jane till Monday morning to let me know. She wouldn't like talk or headlines any better than I. There's something explainable about the whole thing, I'm as sure of it as I can be. Yet—if by that time I don't hear, of course I must begin a search."

"Heavens, man—" Red gazed at his friend with mingled admiration and irritation in his face—"it's all right, I suppose, but I couldn't do it. I'd have the best detective agency I know of working on the case before I went to bed to-night, if it were Ellen."

The shadow of a smile touched Black's lips. "I know you would. Somehow I can't."

"Have you gone through her room? Do you know what she wore, what she took with her? Can you tell what's missing?"

"Perfectly well. She wore what she would wear for any traveling—street clothes and an extra coat. She took a small bag, one she carries when she expects to stay overnight somewhere. Everything's in order about her room and clothes press and desk, as usual. Her window was open—I thought of a breeze's having blown a note into some obscure place, but I've searched every corner. No, whatever she did she meant to do. So you see I have no reason to think she was spirited away by anybody. She went for some good reason, and the explanation's simply failed to reach me."

Well, that was supreme trust in Jane, Red said to himself. Not that he wasn't sure that Jane was to be trusted, yet—human nature is a queer thing, and who knows anybody completely? His thoughts were following this dubious course when it occurred to him to ask:

"Does your housekeeper think you know all about Jane's absence?"

"Yes."

"Then—that stern Scottish conscience of yours must have slipped a cog. The rest of us lie gloriously on occasion, but I never imagined you would."

"I didn't," said Black, with sudden fire in his eye. "I said I expected Mrs. Black back in a few days. I do."

For a moment Red felt an impulse to laugh, but at the next he lost the impulse. There was something superb about Robert Black. He must have come of the blood of the Scotch Covenanters, he decided, to have all that iron in him, in an emergency which differed so decidedly from any ordinary turn of events.

"Well, then," Red suggested, "if you're so sure everything's all right, and don't want my services in starting investigations, why did you say you needed me?"

Black paused in the centre of the room where the two were meeting. "I have to preach to-morrow morning," he said.

"Get somebody else to take the service. You can't put your mind on sermons."

"I can—and will. But—I'm human enough to want you somewhere around, if you can arrange it."

Red's quick smile promised everything.

"You couldn't drive me away. I'll stay till Jane comes walking in, according to your schedule. I'll telephone Ellen—she'll be only too glad to have me here. I won't tell her a thing—won't need to."

So presently Red was stretched upon a couch with cushions wedged high behind his head and a reading lamp at his elbow, pretending to be occupied with a magazine much too far out of his line of interest to hold his attention for a moment. From his shelter he watched Black at his desk—watched and wondered. If Black wasn't concentrating with all his powers on that sermon outline, then Red didn't know concentration when he saw it. The trained and disciplined mind is a thing of which to stand in awe, and Red never felt it more than he did through the hour which followed—an hour and a half it was, actually, before Black put up his notes, his pen, his books of reference, leaving an orderly desk.

Red sat up. His hair was rumpled, but his eyes were alert. Black came over towards the couch, glancing at a clock upon a mantelpiece as he did so.

"I hope you've slept," he said. "I'd no idea it was so late."

"Of course I haven't slept. I kept thinking of a text I heard you preach on once—shall never forget it. *'What, could ye not watch with me one hour?'* "

Black smiled. His face was clear.

"I wonder how many hundreds of hours you've watched beside people who've needed you. Night hours, most of them, too, weren't they?"

"Yes, when the fires die down. But your fires seem to be burning brighter than when I came in."

"Ah, that," said Black, "comes from having you only fifteen feet away from me, even though you might have been asleep."

"I'm going to stay on this couch to-night, by your leave. It's as comfortable as any bed."

"No, you're going to bed, upstairs."

"I want to be within sound of the telephone."

"So do I. And will be. This is my job, Red. I slept here last night."

"Lay awake, you mean."

"No, I did pretty well."

"You won't to-night, with to-morrow and Jane both on your mind. Look here, if you stay in this room I shall too. In that armchair."

They looked each other in the eye. It was a deadlock, and they so recognized it. They both stayed downstairs, and neither of them slept much at all.

As for the telephone, it did not ring.

2

SUNDAY was another day to be got through with. Red found himself aching to have it Monday morning, when the embargo could be lifted and he might go into action. Action—he had planned every detail of it. More than once he had contemplated the possibility of going at it alone secretly, without Black's consent. His friend seemed to him absolutely fanatical in his confidence that everything must be all right. Yet he knew Black wouldn't like it, and it couldn't be done without offending him.

Immediately after breakfast, Mrs. Hodder, who had been Black's competent and devoted housekeeper since the days of his bachelorhood, managed Red into a corner with her finger on her lip. Black had disappeared into his study, and this was an hour when he was accustomed to being quite alone.

"Doctor, could I have a word with you?"

Red was on his guard. Mrs. Hodder was as discreet as a minister's housekeeper should be, but she was a woman. He trusted no woman—except Ellen. They told things—they probably couldn't help it.

"All right, Mrs. Hodder, what is it? A touch of that old lumbago of yours?"

"No, sir. It's—something that worries me more than anything like that. I daren't speak to Mr. Black, but I think you ought to know. It's a bit of —call it gossip—anyway, it's eyes and tongues. I wanted to be able to stop it, and I thought you could tell me."

"Step on its tail, cut off its head, whatever it is. And what is it?"

"Dr. Burns, it's none of my affair that Mrs. Black should be away. God knows she's a fine lady, if ever there was one——"

"Come—out with it, Mrs. Hodder."

She faced his eyes—eyes that could be hawk-like in the way they looked you through. But hers were steady.

"Doctor, I can't help knowing Mr. Black didn't expect to find Mrs. Black away Friday. I came on him accident'ly when he was going through her clothes presses and her whole room and looking behind everything. I went away again—he didn't see me. I kept Della away. He's not been himself since.

And I heard something this morning, from Della, that came from the maid at the Leonards', next door. She saw Mrs. Black go away Friday morning with a man in a big open car—it was a very handsome one, she says."

"Well, good Lord, what if she did! He came after her—his wife was desperately ill and wanted her." (It was the only tall lie he could think of on the instant, not a very convincing one, he realized.) "Will you tell Della to tell the maid at the Leonards' that people go away in big open cars every day—sometimes many times a day. It's very much the custom. And that maids who try to get up talk about such things deserve to have a hole bored in their mean little tongues."

"Yes, sir. Only, if you'll excuse me, I don't think it would be best to say that to Della. She's not been here very long, and she might take offense."

"Let her. Well, I'll leave it to you what to say—only squash that ridiculous suspicion, Mrs. Hodder. Everything's right as rain. Mrs. Black will be back either to-morrow or next day, and that's all about it."

"Yes, sir." But the housekeeper still lingered. "Dr. Burns—you can trust me. I—I think of Mr.

Black—all these years—the way I would a son, if I may say so, and him so far above me. It's going to be hard for him to preach this morning."

The woman was shrewd. He hadn't fooled her. And he did understand her devotion to Robert Black. She had been desolated when he went away to the war—had shed anxious tears. He decided quickly.

"Mrs. Hodder, there's just one thing for you to do. It's absolutely true that Mr. Black expects his wife back very soon. Now, that's all I need to say— or you. Make nothing of her absence—don't let anybody else make anything of it. Get that worried look out of your face. Probably Della's listening at the keyhole right now. That's the way all kinds of hellish gossip starts—people whispering in corners. Don't whisper, even to me. All right—" he raised his voice slightly—"take that prescription and get it filled." He pulled out his pad and scrawled a few words upon it. "Have you any of those brown tablets left from the other attack?"

His eyes warned her, and after an instant's confusion she caught his meaning. She too spoke more audibly.

"Yes, Doctor, I think so. I'm sure I'll be all right in a day or two. I know it's nothing serious, now that you say so. The pain's better already, just talking to you."

His softening glance rewarded her.

But he went away from the corner feeling more uncomfortable than ever.

No matter whom Jane had gone away with, even with his comprehensive knowledge of human weakness, it was incredible that it hadn't a reasonable explanation. But it wasn't incredible that there had been an accident. A big open car—that probably meant speed. If he hadn't learned that Cary Ray was still abroad he might have thought it was he who had come for his sister, for some erratic reason. But an accident—and Jane carrying always a card of identification—they would have heard. Kidnaping —that might be possible. Jane was quite striking in appearance; her clothes, though quiet in style, always suggested wealth in their material and cut, as did the costly furs she wore with them. . . . Her purse—he had an idea it was always well filled. . . .

Bothered and unhappy, even more than he had been before, an hour later he took his place in a pew well down toward the front of the great church, awaiting Black's appearance. He had evaded seeing him before he left the manse; he himself was too much excited.

During the following hour, however, he saw an exhibition of as cool control as ever he had seen in his life. A patient might go to an operating table jesting with his attendants—every now and then one did. But to go into a pulpit before a large audience of sophisticated people, bearing such suspense as was bound to be Black's in spite of all his avowed confidence, could be nothing short of an ordeal. Black had preached once, years ago, two hours after a dislocated shoulder had been reduced by Red, the patient having refused an anæsthetic, and Red had watched him from the pew, as now, and recognized the pluck it had taken. But this was, at least potentially, a worse situation than that had been. Red could hardly sit still in his pew seat; he didn't hear much of the sermon. He did hear the closing hymn, and saw that Black was singing it with his congregation.

> "I thank Thee, Lord, for strength of arm
>   To win my bread,
>   And that, beyond my need, is meat
>   For friend unfed;
>   I thank Thee much for bread to live,
>   I thank Thee more for bread to give."

"No, Mrs. Black isn't ill, thank you—she's away for a few days."

"Mrs. Black is away for the week-end; she'll undoubtedly be back in time for the Women's Guild meeting."

"No, not ill. You're very kind . . ."

"Thank you—she would appreciate your missing her."

And so on. It was Red who barged into it and diverted the sweeping current of questioning. Plague take the women, had some mad story actually got. started that they couldn't crowd up fast enough to bother the minister with their inquiries?

"Excuse me, Mr. Black," said Dr. Burns's slightly imperious voice over the shoulders of the women. "An old friend of yours is waiting in your study, and he has to catch a train in exactly ten minutes. I promised to bring you over in a hurry. You'll excuse him, ladies?"

The group disappointedly made way. When Dr. Burns issued orders, people obeyed, frequently fuming. At the present moment he strode determinedly ahead of Black back down the aisle to the pulpit anteroom, turning to say something over his shoulder with a grin at the minister, to show those who looked after them—as virtually everybody did—that the summons wasn't a tragic one.

"It takes you——" acknowledged Black, as they crossed the green velvet of the late October lawn to the manse.

"Certainly it takes me. This was the one bit of action allowed me. But believe me, Bob, you can't hold me down after to-night."

"I won't try. I found it decidedly harder to keep my thoughts on that sermon than I'd expected. And I hadn't expected it would be easy."

"*Are* you descended from the Scotch Covenanters?" Red demanded.

"Yes. What of it?"

"Everything of it. Stubbornness of it. Doggoned obstinacy of it. Triumph of it, maybe—I admit that."

"So I pray," said Black.

"And so do I—and don't you think I don't."

"I don't think you don't. I know you do."

"But the detective agency——"

"All right, Red—to-morrow."

3

THEY didn't have to wait till to-morrow. It was at ten o'clock that evening that there came a telephone call from New York. Red crowded so close to Black's shoulder that he could hear the voice—he couldn't help it. He listened shamelessly, and after the first sound of that voice he was glad Black was answering, for he couldn't have done it himself at that blessed moment. He heard the whole brief conversation, and the mixture of Irish blood in him beat madly in his pulses for relief.

"Robert, it's Jane."

"Yes . . . dear. . . . Where are you?"

"Why, where I said I'd be—with Cary and Fanny at the Herkimer in New York. They've just come back from Germany."

"I didn't get the message. I'm pretty glad to hear."

"Oh, Bob! Why, I left one. Whatever——"

"Never mind. Tell me what's the matter."

"I can't—not this way. But I want you to take the first train down—will you, Bob? And if you could bring Red—you really must bring Red, if it's possible."

"I can, I'm sure."

("You bet you can," said Red in Black's ear.)

"Bob—you haven't known where I was all this time?"

"Yes, I've known, Jane—somehow."

"Oh—yes, I understand, bless you. I can't tell you anything more, but it's heaven to know you and Red are coming. You see, Bob—I'm in—the other place!"

"Jane, we'll come by air, if necessary."

"Please do. Air will be none too quick. Tell Red if he'll bring you by plane I'll never forget it."

Red took the telephone away from Black. He shouted into it.

"We start in half an hour, Jane. You don't deserve it—but we do!"

Black took the telephone back. "He's a red-head, Jane—but mine is turning that shade. We'll see you in no time."

"Bob—I'm so sorry. Everything's all right—with me. Not—with the others."

"We'll make it right."

"I know you and Red will. It's beyond me. Good-bye—for just a few hours."

"Good-bye, Jane."

The two men turned to each other.

"You win, Bob Black," said Red. His hazel eyes were glistening.

"I think it's my Jane Black that wins," responded Robert Black. As for his eyes—they wouldn't bear looking at. Even the descendant of a Scotch Covenanter has his melting point.

4

INTO action at last went Red Pepper Burns, but into a quite different action from that which he now acknowledged would have been premature. He called up his pilot, he called Ellen, he had a brief session with Mrs. Hodder which left that good woman blinking. In his car he and Black rushed over the miles to the airport and found the plane tuned up, the pilot grinning cheerfully. Being a pilot for the red-headed doctor had very nearly become Norton's mission in life, for a year or so, at least, by which time he would have had a sample of every kind of hasty summons and been allowed to take off in every brand of weather not definitely too perilous. This time it was a still October night, a half moon and no clouds. All right—we were lucky.

To Mitchell Field, eh? That suited him. And they went like an arrow to its mark.

"Like it?" roared Red into Black's ear. He had never had this chance to convoy his friend before.

"It's magnificent."

The great airport, without a stop. A car into New York from there, making quick time in the two o'clock hush of the morning. They drew up before the Herkimer, an old hotel in an unfashionable district where the street was quiet as a village.

In the lobby they registered and had Mrs. Black's room called. They were sent up, their light luggage in the hands of a sleepy-eyed Negro bellboy. In a minute more they were in Jane's private parlor. Red turned his back on the meeting while he feed the boy. Then he turned around again. He was devoted to Jane; he was thankful to see her safe. But his first quick glance told him that she had been through a siege. He knew exactly what sort, if it were Cary Ray who had called her here. Well, he was ready to meet that bleary-eyed young man—if he were bleary-eyed, as he had been when Red had first known him in past years. Couldn't his type of man ever stay reformed? thought Red, none too sympathetically.

"I found the note I thought I left for you," Jane

was explaining from the shelter of her husband's arm. "In my haste I somehow put it in my own hand-bag, along with some other papers. It's not like me to be so careless. And what I've caused you of worry!"

"Not worry," disagreed Robert Black. "Shall we say—perplexity?"

"No, we'll not say perplexity," Red broke in. "He thought he knew how much he loved you before; when he couldn't find you, he really knew how much. There's a difference."

They smiled at him, standing there together. Red said to himself that they were the finest to look at, finest of quality—finest friends—he and Ellen had ever had.

They all sat down, and Jane told her story, speaking rapidly but quietly, while the two men listened, following every word, every small gesture, watching her mobile, attractively strong young face intently. "Cary came for me in a car he had borrowed. He was wild with excitement and misery, unmanageable —you know how he used to be when you both fought for him. I've never seen him like this since, though the last time I did see him, a year ago, I was sure he was drinking heavily again. He denied it. They've been a year abroad. Fanny was furious with him all the way back because he wouldn't take her to Russia —they'd been in Germany for months. She's taken to drinking too much herself—I can't help suspecting drugs, too, though she vows she doesn't touch them. She can't be trusted. Cary seems to care for her still, but they've quarrelled all the time for months, he says, and she threatens to leave him. Since I've been here I've come almost to hope she will. . . .

"He was determined I should come back here with him—said I was the only one who could deal with Fanny. Said he'd got a nurse and set a guard over her in this hotel till he could get me here. He was really—out of hand. I thought I'd better go with him. You were away." Her eyes met her husband's for an instant; she was mostly looking straight ahead at nobody as she talked, quite unlike Jane, and Red understood the tension she was under.

"I couldn't find Mrs. Hodder or Della—and I thought it was just as well, Cary was so noisy. I packed my little bag like lightning, scrawled just a few words to you—I've wondered ever since why you didn't call me, but of course I never imagined you hadn't had my note. We rushed off—I've never gone over any road so fast. We stopped for lunch, and after it, halfway to New York, I realized that Cary wasn't fit to drive. I begged him to let me, but he was angry and refused. Then—we took a terrific skid, and that did bring him to his senses for a minute. We'd almost crashed into a great tree. Some men came up and—well, they got him over into my seat, and I took the wheel. They urged me not to go any farther with him, but I knew I'd better get him back. After that it was easier. He slumped down in his seat with his head over on his chest, and I made the fastest time I dared. I don't think it was much slower than his, but it was—surer. And I managed to keep cool."

Black's hand tightened on hers. He hadn't let it go since he had sat down beside her. Red said something violent under his breath.

"What's that?" asked Black, glancing at him.

"Never mind. I'm saying it for you, too."

"I can say it for myself," replied the Scottish minister. "Go on, dear. God knows I wish I'd been with you."

"Fortunately Cary'd told me his hotel, before he—went off. I brought him there—it was after dusk, and two porters got him up to his room. They were really very considerate. One of them stopped and helped me put him to bed. I stayed with him —Fanny's room was next door, but she was asleep, and her nurse considered she was engaged for Fanny alone—she told me she'd had her hands full. . . . Oh, it's all such a mess!"

"And where in the mess are you now?" Red asked.

"I hardly know. Cary's been in a terrible state, we thought he might be going blind with the stuff he'd bought nobody knew where. But his sight is clearing a little; the oculist we had over to see him says he narrowly escaped. Perhaps you'll think we should have taken him to a hospital, but he and Fanny both fought that, so we've stayed on here. I've gathered that this hotel is a place where plenty of men come to get over their sprees, and the management winks at illnesses like Cary's."

"They're both sleeping now?"

"Yes, it's the first night we've had any rest. But what they'll be in the morning is what I'm anxious about. I think they'll be enough recovered to go on with the terrible strife they've been keeping up. So you see why I wanted you both. I can't imagine what their future's going to be. If there's any turning to

this lane it ought to come now. You're both so wise
—each in your own way."

They didn't bother to disclaim that, their
thoughts were so busy with the problem before them.
But it was three o'clock in the morning, and presently, after they had all the facts before them, Red
said with decision:

"We'd better get what sleep there's time for.
None of us seems to have had much in the last three
nights. Jane needs it most. I'm going to my room—
it's just across the corridor. If anything happens to
stir up either Cary or Fanny, call me. Meanwhile
—good-night, my children."

"Before you go to bed, Red," suggested Robert
Black, "don't forget to say a bit of a prayer. We'll
all need to do that, to-night."

Red paused. "We'd better make 'em good-sized
ones—and loud enough for Him to hear. He might
happen to be pretty busy with other cases like Cary's.
Plenty of 'em, you know."

"I know. But I've always had a feeling that the
lower we speak the more surely He'll hear. It doesn't
take shoutings to reach Him."

Her husband's arm was again about Jane, and she
turned and laid her head against his shoulder, hiding

her face. Red came around upon her other side and caught her hand into his warm grasp for a moment before he went. This was Jane's only brother—the only member of the family left—over whose fate she was suffering. She did need help, both from above and from below. But he knew well enough how she had risen and would continue to rise to all that might be demanded of her.

As Red let himself into his own room he was thinking: "By George, I get away from all that—forget about it—or imagine there's nothing in it. And then Bob Black brings me up with a round turn because he's so mighty sure there is. Well, there needs to be. Life's too much for us, unless we have some sort of Power to draw on. Bob draws on it, all the time. And that's why he's what he is—stronger in all his quietness than I am with all my blustering. Put that in your pipe, R. P.—*and smoke it!*"

Somehow he felt reinforced for the difficult work of the day which was already at its dawning. Some of us call such reinforcement the result of auto-suggestion—self-hypnosis—anything except the supernatural. Some of us—and among them many mighty men of affairs in the great world—call it God.

5

Red sat at Cary's bedside. It wasn't the first time, as he well remembered. Cary had been an eager, brilliant, though dissipated young writer of special articles for the newspapers, as Red had first known him. He was no longer eager, he might be still capable of brilliancy, when his brain wasn't too befuddled, but he looked at this hour as though the years—though he was only in the late thirties—had worn him out. Gaunt, unshaven, wretched in mind and body, he was propped up among his pillows with his eyes hidden behind bandages, a pitiful sight.

"Good of you to come, Dr. Burns," he had murmured as Red took his thin, shaky hand. "You can't do a thing—nor anybody else. I'm down and out for good this time. Not all my fault, but enough. I don't seem to care much. Let me go. I'll be well rid of life."

What Red said to him was little, after all. Cary wasn't strong enough to listen long. He was no subject for rough handling now; his courage and his will were gone from him; judging by his appearance, the feel of his pulse, the sound of his husky voice, he was indeed in a bad way. Red had had long experience in his profession; he didn't always need a sheaf of reports from laboratories, readings of X-ray films, or conferences with specialists to tell him when a man was very nearly beyond help. He sat and looked with keen trained eyes at Jane's brother and knew that he couldn't bluff and bully him into making a prodigious effort to help himself. All he could do was to try to make him feel that he still had friends, that his sister Jane loved him as devotedly as she had always done, that his chance to play the man wasn't all gone, while life was in him. And that Red himself would stand by him, always.

"That's a lot, Dr. Burns—a whole lot," Cary muttered. "More than I deserve. . . . I wish you'd see Fanny. . . . Maybe you could say something. . . . I don't know. . . . We've both been hitting up the pace for a good while now. I guess we're a pair . . . a pair of rotten fools."

"We're all fools, in a way, Cary. The rest of us aren't going to be hard on you because your particular brand of folly has been different from ours. Yes, I'll go and see Fanny. . . . You still care for her, I believe."

"Maybe. . . . She used to be pretty fascinating to me—different. But—we both got to going our own ways. . . . I don't suppose we can ever get together again. She'd be better off without me—and I—she's changed frightfully. . . . So have I. . . ."

His voice broke—trailed off—was still. In a minute more, while Red watched him, he was asleep —the sleep superinduced by the hypnotics that had been given him by somebody to quiet his restlessness and which hadn't yet lost their effect. Red felt his pulse, satisfied himself that this was only sleep, not a failing heart, made the thin figure comfortable, and went softly away, with a sense of the irretrievable. Yet—he had never given up anybody—he had never given up *anybody*—he wouldn't now.

But before he could see Fanny she was beyond his aid or that of any friend. Robert Black and Jane had left her but a moment before, the nurse was on her way back into the room, when all problems concerning her were settled by her own volition. There had been nothing about her half-stupefied condition to make anyone alert for a possible tragedy. But it had come. Fanny had pulled herself from her bed, stood swaying at a tenth-story window, a disheveled figure which several people at opposite windows saw too late, and had toppled down into a courtyard of the hotel which winked at patrons who came there to recover from the effects of their own colossal folly.

6

"SHE was so pretty once," said Jane, very quietly, when she saw Cary's wife half covered with flowers. "So pretty and so gay. She hadn't quite lost it—you can see something of it now. So old—and yet so young!"

"Looking at her," said Robert Black, "makes me think of those words that always come into my mind in hours like this—I can't recall who said them— *'The swift and solemn trust of life.'* "

Red found nothing to say, though his grave, moved face spoke for him. But those words took hold upon his mind and stayed there. That was it— that was what life was—a swift—how swift—and solemn trust. How to be true to that trust—how never to forget for too long that that was what life was. Not to be burdened by the thought—not to be made gloomy by it. To be steadied by it, to see things in their right values. To laugh and dance when laughing and dancing were in order because humanity must have its outlets, but to be capable of straight and sober thinking when the gayety died down. Men talk much in these days, he remembered, about "seeing life whole." Well, that was the way to see it whole—to see not only the material side of everything and to ignore the spiritual, but to give each its place. If poor Cary and Fanny could have done that. . . .

He went back to that other room and wished that Cary were a little boy and he could take him on his knee. Then he might have known what to say.

7

BUT it took Robert and Jane Black to say it—three days later.

"Cary, dear—you're coming home with us. You're going to *stay* with us."

At the breaking point, for he had insisted on being taken to see Fanny laid away and was now back at the hotel—Jane could hardly wait to see the last of that hotel—Cary burst into hysterical laughter.

"Me!" he cried. "Me—in a Presbyterian manse —*me!* The very books on the shelves in that study would shout at me: 'Get out—you're too bad to be here, among us.' The Scotch preacher couldn't write his sermons with me in the house. Let me stay here and rot."

Black laid a hand on the shaking shoulder.

"Lad," he said, "listen to me. There are books on those shelves written by the greatest atheists and agnostics the world has known. Many of them are thinkers and scientists of to-day, who still can find no hope. I haven't kept these out of my library, I've brought them in. To match them—to outmatch them, to my thinking—are the books of other great men, who have hope—they have belief. When you're fit I'll turn you loose in that library—and I'll order anything else you want to read, on any subject. And one day———" He looked at Jane.

"One day, Cary," said Jane, "you'll sit down at Robert's desk and write—something you could never have written before."

"*His* desk," groaned Cary, with his face in his hands. "Not *his* desk! Nor any other. I'm done, I tell you—done—burned out—wiped out—all except burying me."

After all, it did take Redfield Burns to finish it. "Now, listen to *me,* old boy. You're right—you couldn't do a thing at a preacher's desk. You've got to have one of your own. I'll furnish it. Up in our attic at home is a battered old wreck I had in my first office. I never could quite bear to give it away. But I'll give it to you. It's solid yet, though everything's been spilled on it, from glue to nitric acid. It's got a lot of drawers and pigeonholes. It's been hacked with knives—I had an awful habit of cutting a notch on the left-hand upper edge of the top whenever I'd made a particularly awful blunder in my practise. There are notches enough there to cover every slip you ever made. They ought to satisfy you. You could write at *that* desk, Cary, my boy, eh?"

Cary's head was buried in one arm, in his pillow, but after a moment he reached out the other arm, and his thin hand felt for Red's. The warm grasp it instantly met was dynamic in its power to convey the sense of a friend who absolutely understood him. Not Robert Black, sensitive though he was to human need and wiser than most in meeting it—not Jane, devoted, forgiving, comprehending to a degree— could give to this broken spirit that which the red-headed doctor held in the hollow of his hand—had always held. It is indescribable, unmistakable; there is only one thing greater. Black might bring that one thing greater to Cary at some other time, but at this moment it was only Red who could minister to this mind diseased.

Cary went to sleep exhausted but quiet, his hand in Red's.

8

ONE evening, many weeks later, Red came home two hours late for dinner.

"Never mind," he said, "I've had all I want to eat. They insisted on feeding me up before I left."

"Who—where? Red, you look as though you'd just come from a football game," Ellen said, smiling up at him. "Hair on end, flushed with triumph. Tell me about it."

He flung himself down beside her on the couch. His eyes were very bright.

"I've had a bully time—the time of my life. . . . Haven't had so much fun in a year. . . . Nurses fed me—afterwards—three trays they brought round. Nice girls. They wouldn't let me get away. Everybody's been laughing—even the superintendent; she doesn't often let herself go. Even old Griggs, the janitor—I've never known him to laugh. His *risorious* muscles were left out of his leathery face—or atrophied in childhood. Of course, it wasn't an actual laugh he gave me to-night—just cracked the surface a trifle, the old rascal."

"My dear—do tell me. What have you done now? Something particularly atrocious, of course. You're never quite so happy as when you've shocked ever so many people. Of course they were shocked first and laughed afterwards, because you made them."

"How well you know me, my darling! . . . You're a beautiful creature, do you realize *that?* Here—give me a kiss."

She gave it—no woman on earth would have refused it to this man in this mood.

"That ought to hold you a minute or two," he observed, making himself comfortable with various adjustments of his body to the couch and cushions.

"Not very long, I warn you."

"All right. I just want to play with the memory a little before I try to put it into words. You see I can't give you the picture with words. A series of pictures."

He burst into explosive chuckles. Then he sobered.

"After all, it wasn't so very amusing at the start —nor for some time. This is what happened. I'd left the General Hospital and wasn't far from the Maternity and Children's—it was coming on dusk —when the traffic lights pulled me up at a corner, close beside a young woman standing half doubled over by the curb. I caught a groan from her—a certain kind of a groan. Perfectly evident she was just about through with the first stage. I turned my car around the corner when the lights changed and went back to her. She was lost in the city, didn't know where to go. I've enough Italian picked up in practice to get that much from her, but I couldn't get any intelligible address. She'd probably lost it, and couldn't remember, or speak it if she did. I could see by her bundles she was just off the ship."

"Poor thing. But of course you leaped instantly into action."

"I did, indeed. What doctor wouldn't? I called the traffic cop at the corner, and he stayed with her till I could get the car in shape to take her in. I had a lot of stuff with me. He said: 'Going to run her in to the station?'

"I said: 'Not on your life. Where are your eyes and ears, Reilly?'

"He grinned and said: 'Lucky you happened along, Doc.'

"Knew the Maternity was full, but the General is too—I vow we need more hospitals in that town—I've been roaring about it for the last five years. Maternity was nearest, so I took her there. Got her inside. Then I raised hell. Had to. Gosh!—Well, they ought to be used to me!

" 'But we're full, Dr. Burns,' said they—in the office.

" 'Can't help it. Find a bed for this woman somehow. Have her made ready for delivery, pronto.'

" 'But we *haven't* a bed,' they wailed.

" 'Make one. Take her—get her ready. Good Lord, can't you see we've no time for discussing things?'

" 'But where can we *put* her—afterwards?'

" 'I don't know. But find a place.'

" 'We're so overcrowded now we can't——'

" 'Use a stretcher, then. Fix up something. I'm going to get ready—and I'll meet her in the delivery room in ten minutes.'

"I left 'em plain crazy. Somebody'd called Mrs. Griffin, the superintendent, and she was going crazy on another score. She didn't say it, but that hospital has grown pretty snifty about whom it takes in. It comes of one or two women on the Board they have just now. She didn't want this young foreigner off the streets. I got that. She'd suggested that there was time to take her to St. Joseph's. There wasn't. They're even worse overcrowded there, anyway.

" 'It's a pity,' I shouted, 'some sort of saint isn't patron of this place.' I guess that settled it.

"Anyhow, I found the girl ready where I wanted her, and if ever three nurses had worked like lightning those three had—Sykes, Burton, and Gray. They weren't the ones who'd made a fuss—they wanted to take poor little Italy in, God bless 'em.

"Well, in exactly one half hour, if you'll believe me, from the time I pulled up beside that curb, we had a baby on the scene. Ten minutes later we had another." Red was beginning to laugh again. "Fifteen minutes after that——" He now couldn't control his laughter enough to be able to speak, he could only nod in answer to Ellen's mirthful lifted eyebrows.

"Mm-hm-mm-hm——" He choked himself into intelligibility. "Yes, ma'am, three little strangers—as the Virginian called 'em—landed in a hospital where the beds were all filled and the latest arrivals in the babies' nursery were being tucked into market baskets—all but. I thought those girls would die laughing. I certainly had picked up a whole bouquet of rosebuds to present that hospital with. Two of the little squirmers were yipping lustily, but the third Burton had to work over. She did work over it, as though it were needed to carry on the human race. And when she'd swung it and breathed into it and spanked it pink and finally got a small wail out of it, she was as pleased as though it had been her sister's child."

"Where did they find a bed for the mother?" Ellen was enjoying the story in proportion to Red's enjoyment of it.

"One of those darned girls—Sykes—kidnaped a couple of orderlies who think she's the prettiest nurse in the place—she is, their taste is perfect—and got 'em to sneak over her own bed from the Nurses' Building. Said she'd sleep with Gray—in a single bed, mind you. They had it scrubbed, and put it up in a corner they'd found, and screened it in. And there I left little Italy. She's a dark little beauty in her own right, now that her face isn't screwed up in pain, and her eyes are—whe-w! They were going to get an Italian scrubwoman up to find out all she can tell about where her husband is—if any. I really think she has, though. There was a big gold ring on her finger—might have been brass, of course, out of the ten cent store, to save her face. Hope there's a husband—she's going to need one, with three little brats to look after. We'll have to see she's taken care of, if she hasn't one, eh?"

"Of course we will," Ellen agreed. The Burnses were well used to covering emergencies in the lives of Red's charity patients. He had quite as many of those as he had ever had, in proportion to the rich ones; he had never been willing, as he grew distinguished for his skill, to confine himself to the people who could pay him lavishly. Neither, to their everlasting honor, may it be asserted here, are there very many of the famous in Dr. Burns's profession any less willing than he to give for nothing their best wherever there is need.

"When the war was over Mary Sykes looked at the clock and said I ought to be fed. Well, I hadn't had time for lunch, and realized I was starved as a bear. Don't care much for hospital food, by and large, but I wish you could have seen what those girls fixed up. Some of it, I'll bet, cribbed from the supplies for rich patients—private stuff. Three trays, begorry—one for each of the Mussolini triplets, they said. We had a regular *festa,* up there. Mrs.

Griffin came in on it, and I'll be doggoned if she
wasn't smiling too. All the internes filed in for a
look at me eating, and to congratulate me, the young
beggars, on helping fill up the last cranny in the
place. The whole hospital force was laughing, I assure you, at what Dr. Burns had presented to it,
post haste, special delivery, if ever there was one.
And when I came down old Griggs appeared out of
the coal bin or somewhere and mumbled: 'Well,
Doctor, I hear you've been doin' yer best to increase
the poppylation. Didn't you know we had a plenty
here a'ready?' "

As Red grinned again, in memory of the whole
dramatic event, Ellen told herself, as she had many
times before, that while life was in him he would be
the delighted boy when he had perpetrated an antic
like this one. She guessed easily enough that the
little Italian, since this was her first labor, could have
been got in time to the crumbling old St. Joseph's
Charity Hospital, five blocks away from the handsome graystone Maternity and Children's building
where the elect of the city paid big prices for fine
rooms and special nursing; but that the audacious
Red had taken a peculiar and wicked pleasure in
forcing the case into a place which he considered

none too good for the poorest patient in extremity. Her sympathies were all with him, and she exulted with him at his success. Success?—Could anybody have withstood him, there or elsewhere, when he took command? Ask Miss Mary Sykes, Miss Hilda Burton, and Miss Agnes Gray. Ask the orderlies. Ask Mrs. Griffin herself. It was such diversions as these which made life worth living under a roof which saw not only the beginnings of existence but every so often its ends.

9

"Now—I have a tale for you," Ellen said, when Red had settled down, his pipe drawing smoothly, his body relaxed. He was tired, but he never knew that till a big day was over.

"I went in to see Jane to-day," Ellen began, "and Cary, of course. I suppose most of our visits there all these weeks since he came to the manse have been on his account, really, haven't they?"

"No question of it. Nothing more interesting than trying to salvage a wreck like that. The poor fellow's picking up a little. Sometimes I think—well—hate to say it—but Fanny, from all accounts, was more of a total loss than he was. When a woman goes the limit it seems harder to pull her back than a man. If either of them had to snuff out—that brilliant mind of his, if we can get it functioning again, is worth more to this world than her pinhead one. . . . I hope that doesn't sound too hard. . . . Go ahead. I shouldn't be philosophizing when you have something to tell."

"It has to do with that brilliant mind. When I came in Jane met me with a perfectly dazzling smile. I haven't seen her so actually happy since it all happened. She took me straight up to Cary's room. He was lying down just then—she'd made him, after the excitement they'd had. But your old desk was littered with his papers and books—he'd been writing. He had a newspaper in his hand—one of the great dailies, magazine section of the Sunday edition. He had a special article in it."

"Well!" Red was sitting up straight now, his hazel eyes alight. *"Well!* Doggone it, that's front-page news for the Blacks and us, if ever there was any."

"It was front-page news for Cary, though the article was well toward the back of the section. He'd kept it a secret till he could show it to us. It was a start—it proved he could do it again—that was what he kept saying. He hadn't believed he could. But—this is what you'll like to hear, Red. He vowed it was your old desk that did it—and the notches you'd cut when you'd made a bad failure, as you told him. He said he'd kept thinking that when you cut them you'd probably been, for the moment, in as much of a rage at yourself as he'd ever been, because a doctor's mistakes are sometimes so terribly costly. His had been costly enough, he knew, but the thought that you'd undoubtedly been suffering in mind when you cut the notches was somehow a comfort to him. You'd had to get up and go on again, he said. He'd reached the point where he thought he might do that too. Oh, you've no idea how touching it was to see him, in all his weakness, holding that paper in his shaky hand and asking me to take it to you, his thin face quite radiant."

"Have you got it here?"

"Yes. You'll read it right now?"

"Will I read it! Bring it out."

She had it close by, and handed it to him. He read it rapidly, absorbedly, to the end, leaning forward, his elbows on his knees. His face was alive with satisfaction. Had he been a little tired a few moments before? He wasn't now.

He looked up, striking the paper a blow with his fist.

"He's done it! It may not be his top-notch work, but it shows clear thinking, logic, and his old way of putting things that always made his stuff good reading. He's on his way, Len, on his way back—once again. He pulled out of the ditch in war time, but he was younger then. Easier to make any sort of come-back when you're in your twenties. But to do it in your late thirties, as Cary is—well, it just shows that after all there's something in us that's indestructible, if the right forces get at us. You can thank Bob Black for this. Jane too, of course. She's fed him, body and mind. But Bob's fed his spirit. That's Bob's special and particular job."

"And what have *you* done, dear?"

"Me? . . . Nothing. Just jollied and bullied him —made him laugh. I couldn't talk to him about the immortality of the soul."

"Did he need to believe in that?"

"Believe in it! What's the use of trying at all, without it? Get down and wallow in the ditch, as Cary was doing, if this life ends everything. It doesn't. Why, if I didn't think I could go right on for thousands of years bursting in at doorways, trying out experiments in some celestial lab., and generally stirring things up, I wouldn't care a hang what happened to me."

Ellen's eyes were sparkling. "You'll be doing that, Red, thousands of years from now—somewhere."

"I don't just like," said he with mock gravity, "that word *'somewhere.'* It has a dubious sound. . . . See here, I'm going to telephone Cary and tell the boy what I think of him. There's a branch phone in his room, isn't there?"

"Yes, but it's half-past ten. They don't let him sit up late. He's probably in bed and asleep."

"He won't be asleep—not after putting this over. It won't hurt him to hear me roar at him."

In a minute or two he had the call through. The Blacks were out, the maid Della responded, but Mr. Ray was in. She would connect him with Dr. Burns. Then Red spoke:

"Cary—that you, old boy? See here—I've just been reading that article of yours. . . . Yes. . . . And I'm pleased and proud as if I'd done it myself. . . . It's the real stuff. . . . Oh, yes, it is—and it marks the turn of the tide, or I'm no old sea dog of a doctor. I've no more worries about you. . . . No,

I'm not playing up—you know better. . . . Listen
—did you write that at my old torn-eared bulldog
of a desk? . . . Then I'm prouder yet. Don't cut
any notches in it. Have a bronze tablet set into it.
*'Here's where Cary Ray wrote the first of the most
important series of . . .'* Oh, lie down and pull up
the covers and go to sleep, if you can't take a man
at his word. I'll be in in the morning, on my way to
the hospital, and feel your pulse. If it isn't a fine
average normal I'll count my own—and we'll consider the mean of the two a correct reading. . . .
Good-night, Cary—good-night."

Red hung up the receiver. But before he could
turn away to make a comment to Ellen it rang again,
in his ear. "If that's a call out," he said threaten-
ingly, "here's where I refuse it flat. . . . All right
—*Dr. Burns.*"

And here he presently became a riot. Ellen could
only listen to him and smile. Such a boy he was, at
forty-five—such a dear, engaging, yet mature and
responsible boy! He was kneeling up on the couch,
boy fashion, reaching over to the table behind it
where the telephone stood, bringing it to him without changing his position. She rejoiced in his sturdy
thighs, his solid calves. . . .

"What? . . . That you, Miss Sykes? Go ahead, my dear girl. . . . Of course you're not bothering me. . . . Do I want to *know!* Try telling me. . . ."

Ellen could hear a distant low voice, recounting some tale to which as he listened Red responded with various unintelligible but jolly sounds, while his face became beaming. Then he burst out:

"Miss Sykes, you're a peach. . . . You're all peaches over there—including Her Royal—you know. Gosh!—to have got that solved by this time you must have done even quicker work than I did—beaten my record by a neck. . . . Wish I'd been there. . . . See here, I'll bring flowers when I come in the morning—or some spaghetti—which do you think they'd prefer? . . . Yes, I've got to be in on it. I take that back about the spaghetti—it's flowers she shall have, the little Italy—you're right. Thank you for calling me—thank you—you know when to ring a poor doctor up—it's when you've got something darned important to tell him. . . . Good-night, Mary Sykes."

He swung himself around on the couch to face Ellen.

"My dear, we're going to a wedding in the morning. Yes, you'll have to go too. There never was a

wedding like this one. Little Italy's lover left her
eight months ago to come over here for work. He
didn't send for her, though he'd promised to, but he
wrote to her, and he did give her his address. He
didn't know about what was coming, he says, and I
guess maybe he didn't. But when she was eight
months gone she got a little money together and
came over to find him. . . . Think of that journey,
alone. There's trust in man, for you! But Tony
deserves it.

"The Italian scrubwoman saw the little picture
of him the girl had on a ribbon inside her clothes—
she recognized him. He was boarding near her
home, in the Italian quarter. She brought him to
the hospital this evening—after hours—she had to
sneak him in, but she got hold of Sykes, and she did
some sneaking, too, and got him to see the new
mother and the three little strangers. Mrs. Griffin
got wind of it somehow, though nobody knows how,
but she winked at it, and all was well. That woman
isn't *all* discipline. I'll hand her that. And now, here
comes the tassel on the cap of the story.

"According to Mary Sykes, with the scrubwoman
as interpreter, this was Tony's decision:

"He hadn't got a very paying job—ditch digging

—wouldn't have thought he could marry Rosa if she'd had only one baby. But since she had three—Santa Maria!—*three*—and he admitted they were his—he thought he'd have to help her with them. She was a beautiful girl—and brave—he did love her—he'd bring the Italian priest in the morning."

Red's face was a study as he demanded, between amusement and sympathy:

"Len, since the world began, do you think any man's married a woman *because* she had three babies instead of one?"

"I don't think so. Poor Tony—what a load of care!"

"Rich Tony. Do you mean to tell me three children don't make a man richer than one? What about our three?"

His gay look and question challenged her, as many another look and question of his had challenged her throughout their married life, to answer him honestly and agree with him if she could—or tell him convincingly where he was wrong.

She couldn't dispute him to-night. There seemed to be everything to make him happy to-night. Let him be so—since before morning that same telephone might summon him to some dim place where there was no laughter, only tears. Because these rapid changes made up life—his life, and hers, and everybody's. Yet, somehow, life was worth the living. It had to be.

10

THE telephone did ring again that night—it was at exactly midnight. Ellen and Red were just about to leave the room where they had been sitting talking things over, luxuriating in their quiet companionship.

"Damn!" said Red Pepper.

He wouldn't take the call—he didn't go out nights any more—get somebody else—no, he wouldn't go—they were the worst deadbeats in town. (He was getting madder all the time. He was going to hang up if they didn't stop begging. He didn't hang up, he kept on listening.)

They'd tried to get somebody else—they couldn't find anybody else—yes, they did owe everybody in town—Joe hadn't been able to get work for months —maybe he *was* lazy but he'd tried—part of the time, anyway. The child was sick—awfully sick— they didn't know what to do—what *could* they do, Doctor—he strangles so—oh, please come for the love of the Blessed Mother Mary—think if it was your own, Doctor. . . .

The quick-fire anger went out of him.

Men like Dr. Burns can't, for the life of them, help coming when you call.

THE END

The greatest pleasure in life is that of reading. Why not then own the books of great novelists when the price is so small

¶ *Of all the amusements which can possibly be imagined for a hard-working man, after his daily toil, or in its intervals, there is nothing like reading an entertaining book. It calls for no bodily exertion. It transports him into a livelier, and gayer, and more diversified and interesting scene, and while he enjoys himself there he may forget the evils of the present moment. Nay, it accompanies him to his next day's work, and gives him something to think of besides the mere mechanical drugdgery of his every-day occupation—something he can enjoy while absent, and look forward with pleasure to return to.*

Ask your dealer for a list of the titles in Burt's Popular Priced Fiction

In buying the books bearing the A. L. Burt Company imprint you are assured of wholesome, entertaining and instructive reading